THE GREEN
ENCLAVE

RUNA 7

THE GREEN
ENCLAVE

RUNA 7

JAYE SARASIN

© Jaye Sarasin, 2017

Published by Parfoys Press

www.parfoyspress.com

A CIP catalogue record for this book is available from the British Library.

ISBN 978-0-9957151-0-3

Book layout by Clare Brayshaw

Prepared and printed by:

York Publishing Services Ltd
64 Hallfield Road
Layerthorpe
York YO31 7ZQ

Tel: 01904 431213

Website: www.yps-publishing.co.uk

In memory of Denis

Chapter 1

He heard the patter of hurrying feet and then the distant shouting behind him. The houses were racing past, ancient buildings leaning drunkenly in above him, the jutting upper floors supported on wooden beams almost touching over his head. And the stench was gut-wrenching. He was running, running away from the voices, hearing the far off howling. 'Death to the aristos! Death to the aristos!'

He had come into a narrow alleyway, the dusk of evening revealing behind him, as he glanced over his shoulder, the gleam of distant torches. He stumbled and, looking down, he saw his ragged clothes and then, at the end of the torn sleeve, the tell-tale, all-betraying hint of lace at his wrist. He fumbled at it while he ran but the glove hampered his efforts and he gave up, fleeing into the darkness of the alleyway, hearing in panic the fast-closing baying, 'Death to the aristos! A la Bastille!'

The buildings had an odd grainy look to them – his terror, he suddenly thought, deforming his vision. And then, in an instant, turning a corner, he was at the end of his alleyway and catapulted into a larger street where a thousand rushing bodies jostled him back against the wall and then swept him, puppet-like, along in their midst, shouting and screaming as they headed for the walls of the Old City.

Carried on the surge of the throng he was unable to escape, trapped in the thick of the mob, the faces of the people beside him caught in the flare of the torches. He heard the names of Marat, Danton and Robespierre tossed from one to another exultantly. 'A new society! Freedom and brotherhood! A la Bastille!'

They were not, after all, after him, or perhaps this was a new band. There was a young man next to him with blackened face and grimy, ragged clothes, one torn sleeve of his jerkin flapping in the wind as he ran, white teeth blazing in the dark face. 'We will free them,' the boy shouted. He smiled back, suddenly exhilarated, and forgetting his fear shook his fist and yelled with the others, 'A la Bastille!'

They burst into the concourse and through the gates and then the great grey building was towering over them, bringing them to a juddering halt. He thought of all the poor souls who had disappeared within its walls thirty, forty, fifty years ago, never to be seen again. Now some, at least, would be free.

The bodies crowding round him, the rough unshaven faces, the tattered tricolore streaming in the wind above them, all had an unreal air, and he felt dizzy. The stench had become even more overpowering. The crowd was rushing the gates, using a battering ram. Two men at the front, incredibly brave, were carrying it forward as guards came pouring out and the first man staggered back under the thrust of a pike, red spreading across his chest.

He watched horrified as the crowd surged forward again, the weight of their numbers overwhelming the guards. He had been thrust forward, right to the very front, next to the dying man and looking down saw the splash of red on the lace at his wrist. Another man next to him looked down also.

'Eh, les enfants, it's a dirty aristo here. Who else wears fine lace shirts?' The voice was thick with anger and disbelief.

He looked around alarmed, saying, 'No, no, I stole it,' but saw that they did not believe him, the boy's face also shading with anger. He ducked, moving quickly back into the crowd, pressing his hand into his glove. The furious murmurs began to swell, the hatred feeding on hatred.. 'A dirty aristo! Where? Where?'

He thrust his way through to the mob's edge, the man still close on his heels, his shadow thrown before him by the torches, showing the knife lifting in his hand.

He pressed his hand into the glove more desperately, heart pounding, throat dry with wracking terror. He made the pistol shape and pointed desperately skyward, pressing, pressing the button in the glove.

It was not responding. And the man's face, huge, grainy looking, like fine woven linen, was on top of him, the bad teeth above him, the hatred filling his whole field of vision as the man screamed, 'Filthy aristo, kill him, kill him!'

A gleaming blade with red upon it scythed towards his throat, he twisted desperately under the man's hand and suddenly he was up and free, soaring into the velvety sky, above the crowd in turmoil below, the lights of the torches becoming small pin pricks of light in the distance. Turning his head downward he could see the scene below him grow smaller and smaller, the crowd now like ants as he travelled away from them, up into the dark sky.

Then the blackness before him was overlaid with writing as the lesson concluded.

The storming of the Bastille took place on 14 July 1789, Paris, France (former regional name of the western part of Runa Four)... End of the monarchy etc, etc …

Yes he knew all that. He recognised the names that he had heard being shouted, Robespierre, Danton and Marat, men who had been responsible for sending so many to the guillotine. It seemed incredible that so few people could have been allowed so much power and could have caused such terror. It was infinitely better now.

'Sez who?' Stick Michaelis had said when they had talked about it in tutorial but Stick had been born cynical.

A notice came up saying 'Now make your notes. Your notefile is on your terminal', and he made the required clenched fist gesture to stop the program. The images faded and the world went black.

He took off the headset, blinking a little in the natural light from the window, unbuttoned the data glove and unclipped the sensors from his wrist and arm. His heart was settling down to its normal rhythm. History lessons in cyberspace were ace, especially when you had such high definition and the sensors responded to your every movement and emotion. After a lesson like that he was never likely to forget what it must have been like to be an aristocrat in France during the French Revolution.

It was clever the way they had made the computer refuse to respond to the glove instructions at the end there. It had been really terrifying when it had not answered his call to escape. No doubt the program reacted to information from the sensors and, depending how frightened you were, responded accordingly.

The headset contained the laser which projected images directly onto the retina. It was a great improvement on the small screens which virtual reality had relied upon until recently. It was a really ace set. His dad had given it to him for his birthday. He felt he would have no trouble with the exams now.

'Me look, Jake,' came the small voice.

Emma had come toddling into his room and demanded to try the headset and so he found a fairy story card and fed it into the computer for her. The dataglove was made of a highly elastic material with fibre optic cables sandwiched between the layers of fabric and it adapted fairly easily to Emma's little hand. At the base of the glove was a sensor which tracked your position and the direction you were looking in and altered the screen view. If you turned your head to the left you saw a scene from the left, when you moved towards an object on the screen it grew bigger. The sense of touch had been created by placing vibration sensors inside the fingertips of the glove.

'Me want to fly,' said Emma.

'Point your finger,' said Jake. 'Point where you want to go. Make a gun shape, bend your thumb.'

'Whoops,' she said.

Manoeuvring in cyberspace was an art. At first you blundered about like a wasp in a jam jar, crashing through walls and banging your virtual elbows on every virtual object. When you reached forward to pick up a pencil off the floor you went straight through the carpet. If the lesson were good enough and you were experienced enough, however, you did not notice at all that the world was not real.

Emma chuckled. 'Fluffy bunny,' she said.

Jake took out the small closed tray on the side of the machine and replaced the crystals which had been used during the lesson. Strictly speaking called the OSC or Olfactory Sensation Chamber but known to all as the Smelly Box it allowed different crystals to be released at the required moment, dissolving on contact with the air, producing the right scent. The attempt to reproduce the extremely pungent odours of eighteenth century France must have sorely tested the skills of their smell chemists, thought Jake and, remembering the awful pong of rotting cabbage mixed with pee if not worse, he decided they had made a very good fist of it. He lodged the smelly box back into its slot.

Checking the time he said firmly, 'Right, Em, that's it.' You had to be very careful with small children and virtual reality. The flicker of the images in the old sets had sometimes triggered small brain seizures, minute in themselves but dangerous over a longer period. Sets were better now, of course but ten minutes was the recommended dose for a three year old.

'Just see the stoopid prince,' she said pleadingly. Em thought the prince was stupid because he kissed the princess instead of pulling her pigtails which was Em's idea of a sensible course of action.

'OK,' said Jake, watching it on the second screen and getting ready to turn it off the instant the prince kissed the princess.

The princess suddenly fell backwards from the wall she was sitting on so Jake guessed Em had helped the prince out with the pigtails. He extracted her protesting from the dataglove and headset.

'Want to fill the smelly box,' she complained.

'I've already done it, Em. And it's time you went to bed.'

'You're a SWIP,' she said darkly.

'What's a SWIP?'

'Silly Wally with Pimples.' Em was feeling hard done by.

Jake grinned. 'You know you're supposed to be in bed,' he said, packing her off to her bedroom and disconnecting. He made a few rough hand notes and then sat back frowning.

The lesson had almost made him forget the reason why he was doing schoolwork. His dad had not come. This was bad but not so bad as the fact that he hadn't texted or e-mailed to say what was up. He had just not come. And tomorrow his mother would be off again and Margie would come round and his dad would not come for another fortnight. It was all very depressing. Far away he heard a phone chirruping and he waited for a few moments to see if his mother would page him to join in the call but she didn't so it was probably someone from work.

He went down to the kitchen but by the time he got there she had switched the phone off and was slicing the bread for his sandwiches the following day. She was absorbed, her close cropped head bent over the loaf, the neat methodical strokes producing slices of perfectly equal thickness. It was typical of his mother's efficiency that, he thought, and even as he thought it the knife suddenly slipped and in an instant there was a long red line on her hand with a small dark bubble on the end.

'Oh rats,' she said and then grabbing a paper towel and holding it tightly to the cut digit, 'Get me the skinseal, Jake, will you?'

The red began to show through the paper towel.

'How dumb,' she said faintly and Jake said cheerfully 'Aren't you just?' as he grabbed the skinseal tube and a small bottle of disinfectant from the cupboard. Turning he saw with surprise that she had gone quite white and he sat her down in the chair before wiping the finger and rubbing some disinfectant on.

'Not my efficient mother at all,' he said holding the two edges firmly together and running the skinseal along the cut.

'Ouch, you don't have to be so rough' she said shakily and then slightly more firmly, 'It's all right, it's only a cut.'

'Was that Harry?' he asked, despising himself, knowing that it wasn't.

She was holding the two edges of the cut together tightly, her expression distracted. Years ago he might have hoped that she was disappointed that his father was not coming but since the arrival of the new man and Emma he had given up any hopes on that score.

'Your father?' she said vaguely and then, more slowly, 'Mm. He sends his apologies, he was in a rush. He couldn't come today; he'll probably come next week instead.' Her voice was still shaky as she patted the remaining blood away from the finger. 'And I'm off at six tomorrow, so I've got some work to catch up on'. She rubbed her forehead.

'Did he say why?' he asked.

'No, no, just one of his trips, I think.'

She was obviously not concentrating. His father worked in a parallel section to his mother's at the same boring government department, although his father had a much lower ranking. She was some sort of legal beagle, checking tariffs for the bigger multi-nationals for the Ministry of Trade and Agriculture and they were always being called to some far flung spot.

'Are you going to the same place?'

'No, I'm off to Runa Seven, heaven help me. Steven will probably look in on you and, of course, Margie will come.'

'There's been a lot of bad news on the web about Runa Seven. They said things about "unexplained deaths" and "damage to the Enclaves" and so on.' He paused. 'Some of them said it was the League of the Dead.'

His mother's face relaxed into a smile. 'You know they're just a fairy story, Jake. I'd be more likely to be chased by the Bogeyman. No …' her expression hardened. 'Real people are responsible. It's true that Runa Seven is bad news at the moment, but don't you worry. I won't be involved with that end of it.'

'I wasn't worrying,' he said, stealing one of the sandwiches and earning himself a black look.

Back in his bedroom Jake thought about his mother going to Runa Seven and liked the idea even less. It had a very bad reputation and there had been a lot in the news about it recently.

Perhaps that was what was upsetting her, he thought, although he knew his mother was always extremely careful in these places. And he wished that she had paged him so that he could have joined in the conversation with Harry on his own phone. He quite liked Steven, Em's dad, who lived in the next unit to theirs, but it wasn't the same A horrible thought suddenly occurred to him and he rushed off to look in the bathroom mirror.

Surely he didn't have pimples?

Chapter 2

He made a mental note to check with security for last minute ERC instructions as he left the condo. It was good to get out of the village even if only for a day, away from the security systems, the guarded gates, the sense of enclosure. Today was ERC day and the prospect of seeing all his friends. It was a laugh to call it an Educational Resource Centre when it was just a few crumbling buildings and a set of tatty old computers, but it did mean he'd get to see Allie. He'd be able to ask if she'd downloaded the same history lesson.

He had said farewell to his mother much earlier as she left for Runa Seven. She had seemed pale and tired in the morning light, her neat short black hair swept back, wearing a crisp shirt with impeccably starched collar under the sober navy blue trouser suit. She was small and dark like him, with a slim brown face, black hair and vivid brown eyes, also like him. He took after his mother not his blond father. Em's father was tall and blond too (must be the sort his mother went for he had decided) and Em was like him, a large, loose, floppy child, with a peaches and cream complexion. In personality she too was like her father, good natured and amiable; she loved flowery pants suits and playing with her dolls, much he thought to his mother's disgust. His mother favoured a more severe style.

This morning she had looked particularly official with the small briefcase chained to her wrist by the tiny chain. It didn't look particularly strong but his mother assured him that they'd be able to get her arm off more easily.

She was off to Runa Seven for a week at least and Margie was installed. He wondered if he could have another go at explaining to his mother how he hated Margie but she had seemed distracted and had been more concerned with making sure that he collect her laundry at the end of the week.

'Go for it without fail on Friday, if I'm not back,' she had said repeatedly. 'It's important. I've left a reminder on Charley Sank.' Charley Sank was the main computer which ran most of the equipment in their unit, the internal security system, the energy conserver, the answer phone, the piped oxygen and so on.

'Your dinners are numbered. Don't let Margie get them out of order. Pay your history magazine subscription. It's due.'

The orders crackled out and it was easy to imagine her at work, marching down corridors with dedicated purpose, not so much opening doors as crashing through them. His father had said to him ruefully one day that in a previous incarnation Vanessa had been a hand grenade.

It only took five hours to Runa Seven. 'I'll give you two short rings to your wristcom when I get to Kinshasa so that you'll know I'm OK.'

'Don't do anything rash,' he had said, as he always did, hearing the Ministry shuttle beep on the intercom, and she had given him a quick kiss and, rather surprisingly, a hug and was gone.

He checked the ozone monitor and decided that the cream was going to be insufficient today – he would have to wear his visor. The ozone was supposed to be reconstituting itself but it wasn't evident.

As he left the gatehouse the oxygen pack on his left upper arm began to click and puff slowly. People were still dying, even so many years after the Blind Ages, with breathing complaints and the desperate shortage of oxygen in the atmosphere. Condo dwellers had, of course, central piped oxygen and the pack only became useful when you went out into the open. And here, so close to a Green Enclave, the air was noticeably better than down town Kington anyway.

He got to the lightrail station with seconds to spare, the oxygen pack on his upper arm puffing and clicking with all the extra effort required by the running, drip feeding its life-giving gas through the little pad on his left breast. Allie laughed at him as he leaped aboard next to her just before the train pulled away.

'Come on, slugabed.'

He grinned at her. She grinned back and his heart lurched sideways as it always did at the sight of her smile. They stood companionably side by side in the central gangway, strap-hanging, as two guards pushed past them, making their usual inter station patrols.

'Do you think there'll be any problems today?' he asked.

'Nah,' said Allie, unconvincingly. 'There never are on Mondays. The Staters are all wiped out after the weekend.' Her long fair hair swung across a face suddenly grown thoughtful.

On one side of the lightrail on a distant hill was the Green Enclave with its totally impassable defences. There was never any danger from there. Beyond the bare strip of land and the wire and the unseen electronic shields the huge trees rose in massed ranks for mile on mile, beautiful against the washed out blue of the sky.

It was from the other side that the danger came, the four or five miles along Thorp Edge before Crater Hill. It was particularly bad on the section leading to the Crater Tunnel. He had his bribe money, of course, so even if anything happened he was probably all right. Still, you never knew.

He grinned at Allie, knowing that his face looked uncoordinated and stupid. 'Did you get a good history lesson?' Why was it that he was unable to think of anything witty or original to say when he was with her?

Allie made a face. 'Nah. All about the Eringaard laws and the foundation of Runa Two. All red Indians and cowboys and how they bought New York for a handful of beads. The usual old legends. What is it today?'

'Just the tutorials I think. And then footie. Then there's the eco-science lecture this afternoon.'

'Just a load of old junk.' said a weedy youth as he moved past them down the carriage. 'Trying to convince us they can turn the clock back.'

Allie raised an eyebrow as the youth disappeared into the next carriage.

'He's just s SWIP,' said Jake, and then, as Allie looked questioningly, 'Silly Wally with Pimples.'

Allie's eyes twinkled. 'Em?'

Jake nodded.. Yes. Heavens knows what Mum will say when she finds out how Em's learning the alphabet at that place.'

Allie laughed, pushing the fine blond hair back from her face and smiling at him. 'They grow out of it. And regardless of the SWIP I quite enjoyed the last lecture. They had someone in from Ecoproguardia.'

'What? Ecopro?

'Yes, that's it's real name apparently. Their lecturer was really enthusiastic. It made quite a change.'

He nodded agreement and glanced out of the window at the unyielding green line of the Enclave. The lightrail slowed down considerably on the steep slope up to Crater Hill and he felt the habitual niggling worry. Recently Staters had taken to dropping onto the roof from the top of the cutting and jemmying open a couple of freight doors. This set off the emergency stop system and allowed one or two Staters to board the train, smashing their way through to the passenger compartments. The ultra lightweight materials compulsory on all moving vehicles except international trains were no proof against Stater sledgehammers.

He suddenly remembered the envelope in his pocket. He had grabbed the post from the security box at the entrance on his way out, taken his History magazine and, most unusually, a letter addressed to himself out of the pile and thrown the rest back in. Nobody sent letters these days except legal ones for government departments. There were several for his mother but they would have to wait till she returned. Her secretary would take care of the business ones. He had had no time to open his own letter since he had wanted to catch the early lightrail with Allie and so had shoved them both into his bag and then forgotten them. It was the effect Allie had on him.

Now he took a quick look at the History magazine but did not bother to open the letter. It was probably just the usual feeble excuses for not coming on Sunday. He was surprised that his father had bothered to send it by post. Usually it came by email or podcast along with the morning news extracts. He was just shoving it into his pocket when the train screeched to a halt.

A few seconds later there was a terrible hubbub from the far end of the car. Somebody screamed. The connecting door to their carriage slammed back and the two Staters stepped in; one, a large strongly built young woman dressed in dungarees, and the other, a thin, white-faced youth following nervously behind her. They were both brandishing stun guns and the woman was holding a battered plastic box in front of her.

She shook it and the money and jewellery in it rattled.

'Come on, people,' she jeered. 'Contributions to the Crater Edge Hospital Fund. You don't want to have to sample the treatment, do you? We just want a little contribution.'

She thrust the box under the noses of people down the car and they dropped their money in sullenly, not saying anything, watching the waving stun gun in a wary manner.

She was shaking the box in front of an old lady.

'Oh, come on, woman. You can do better than that. What about that nice ring you're wearing.'

The other passengers watched as the old lady tried to get the ring off a knotted finger, all looking as if they would like to say something, to protest, but afraid to. Jake and Allie dropped their bribe money silently into the youth's box. About two minutes had passed, thought Jake. The security guards should arrive at any minute.

The old lady was beginning to panic as the stun gun waved closer and closer. 'It's my wedding ring, she was saying pleadingly, still tugging at her finger. 'You surely won't take my wedding ring. I haven't had it off for years. It won't come off.' The Stater was getting impatient and beginning to glance down the car.

'I'll chop it off, finger and all, you stupid old cow,' she hissed, 'if you don't get a move on.'

The desperation on the old lady's face was stark. Stun guns were only supposed to render you unconscious but for the old they could be fatal. She had got the ring actually on the knuckle and the Stater was grabbing at it, her attention and that of her companion in one second deflected as the security guards came running in.

The woman looked up, swore violently, and leapt for the door nearest to her just as the emergency override swung into place and the doors began to close. She was through and then the thin, undernourished young man after her, pale white despairing face disappearing backwards as the kick of the guard's gun blew him out of the train.

'He's hit the edge of the tunnel,' said someone excitedly. 'He's a gonna, that's for sure.'

'Serve him right,' another voice said.

'Are you all right, love?'

Everybody was consoling the old lady and feeling relieved that they had escaped so easily.

'It's absolutely terrible the way they can just smash their way onto these trains. The Administration should be doing something about it.'

'Fat hope of that. They've got enough on their hands just keeping the security corridors open.'

'He was just young, they shouldn't have killed him,' said Allie suddenly. 'And he didn't look as if he got enough to eat.'

'Probably because he spends all his money on crack and white crystal,' said an old man next to Jake. Jake agreed but he knew that Allie was a softie. She belonged to all sorts of organisations that helped the disadvantaged.

'I don't suppose he meant to kill him it was just his bad luck that he hit the edge of the tunnel.'

'It's their living conditions,' said Allie hotly. 'You can't expect much when people have to live like that.'

There was a waver of lights as the electricity, drained by the emergency stop, came back up to full strength. The opinion of the carriage by and large was that the Stater had only got what was coming to him. Someone opined that the guard must have used a hard gun instead of just a stun gun and Jake thought this was quite likely.

'They don't need to live like that. If they just managed carefully on what the government gives them. Some have even got jobs.' The speaker was a middle aged man with a bull neck and a flushed red face.

'Others steal it off them. They don't have proper security systems,' said someone trying to be fair.

'They don't have proper hospitals or anything,' said Allie, still annoyed.

'They don't need to take it out on innocent old ladies though, do they?' said the red faced man shrewdly.

It was unanswerable. Allie's face flushed slightly and Jake could see that she was going to get them into hot water. He pressed her arm warningly and she looked at him and then shook her head in impatience but said nothing.

Jake looked round the carriage. Most here, he would have thought, were condo village dwellers as he was, with their high walls, guards and security systems – the only ones with enough money to travel the train.

They were not happy with Allie. 'Some people don't know when they're well off,' said the old lady querulously.

A thin waspish young woman, obviously a leader by her dress and manner, said loudly, looking accusingly at Allie, 'Some people would just give these young thugs anything.'

Allie lifted her chin defiantly and said 'How would you like to have been born in a Stater town?' but the feeling was running against her.

'Perhaps you should have been,' said the woman.

Jake would like to have said something cutting, something which would put the woman in her place, which would have demonstrated to the disapproving carriage that Allie was in the right, even though he did not agree with her, but could think of nothing suitable.

'We'll end up having to get the sky-train in the end,' said someone else, fortunately changing the subject.

'They brought one of those down last week with a couple of drones,' said the bull-necked man. 'Luckily those SiliconBH shell carriages are pretty good and it isn't as if they fly very high, so nobody was killed, but it's soon going to be a nightmare getting across to Kington.'

Luke gazed down moodily at the floor. Suddenly he thought of his letter and fumbled in his pocket, finding it eventually tucked inside the history magazine. He tore open the flap and peered in, seeing only an old lesson card. He must have left it at Harry's the last time he'd been there and Harry had just shoved it into an envelope and sent it by office post to save the money. He couldn't remember leaving anything. He had a few moments before the start of the tutorials and the terminals were available at any time. He'd try out the card before going to the Maths tutorial to see what it was.

The line turned aside from the Green Enclave and headed for Kington and the ERC stop. The splendid scenery of the Enclave and the bare, rock-strewn landscape of Crater Edge on the other side of the track, gave way to the hideous barricaded walls of small condo villages, the blazing gleam of the distant glasshouses and the inevitable, omnipresent mustard-brown weed, the only thing that could survive the sun's light. On some trips Jake thought he had caught sight of an odd patch of green here and there as the chemical imbalance began reversing and small amounts of chlorophyll survived the sun's deadly rays, but here in uptown Kington none was visible. And then they had reached the jumble of buildings that preceded Kington and the light rail slid into Kington ERC.

Chapter 3

He waved goodbye to Allie in the central hallway as she went off to her psychology tutorial. A funny little woman came in from the Medical Resource Centre before surgery and so Allie started lessons before anyone else. His tutorials in History and Maths didn't start until ten so that left him enough time to take a look at the lesson which his dad had sent him.

He managed to get one of the last cubicles with a terminal in the private study section of the ERC. So much for Educational Resource Centre – not too many resources these days and most of the equipment either broken or quite out of date. He took the envelope from his pocket and looked again at the card, finding a small slip of paper with it which he had not noticed before.

The message said: 'Sorry I didn't phone. You forgot your lesson card, Dad.'

This did not make Jake feel a lot happier. The briefest of apologies, no matter that they had arranged to go to the movies, no matter that Harry knew that he had put off a special history trip just to be with him. He wondered if it was Harry's thoughtless way of treating people that had discouraged his mother. And he was pretty certain that he hadn't forgotten any lesson cards. It probably belonged to the stupid kid belonging to the woman Harry was seeing pretty frequently.

He'd look at it anyway before he did the math. He typed in his ERC password which allowed him access to the Centre's operating system, slid the card in and then banged the Card Key. The machine whirred gently.

'Please log in.'

He typed in his password again and waited for the machine to respond. The screen flickered and then went blank. He must have got another duff lesson. He took it out in irritation, shoved it back in and typed in his password again. Perhaps he had made a mistake. He banged the Card Key four times and suddenly the machine whirred again and then said courteously: 'Please check your password.'

He took the card out and looked at it. It was just an ordinary lesson card, with HISTORY on the name tape. The actual title was scuffed and unreadable. This meant that it was a pupil card probably containing an information section which was on a hidden file along with questions, research projects, interactive video and so on and then open files for the pupil's response.

He reinserted the card and tried a general password used in the event of system breakdown. The screen stayed resolutely blank. It must belong to the other kid. He went to another ERC and they probably had a different operating system.

He took the card out again and inspected it. Lesson card programs were virtually indestructible. When the home education system had first started children were always saying blithely, in order to excuse their missing homework, 'I just pressed the wrong button and it wiped,' but now that was almost impossible. Only really gifted hackers like Stick Michaelis could break into the school lesson card system without it showing. But Stick very rarely used his talents on school lessons. He wouldn't tell you how to do it either. He'd take the card away and bring it back wiped and that was that. Apart from the payment that was.

Jake was preparing to tuck the card back into his card holder when he saw that the corner of the name tape was a little out of line and that another tape showed above it. Somebody had stuck a new name tape on. A school history lesson tape. He pulled at it but only succeeded in bringing the tape underneath off as well.

He looked at the lesson card again and then at the note and suddenly felt slightly uneasy. His father never signed himself Dad. He signed himself Harry, which was his name. Harry Stanford Farnol. There was something wrong. And this wasn't a lesson card. It seemed slightly lighter and frailer than a lesson card which was built to resist school life.

His dad had sent him this card? Why? Was he trying to send him a message? If so he must know he couldn't read it.

The centre's holocoms were usually out of action so it wasn't worth trying them, but he had his wristcom. He tried his dad's work's number first.

'Good morning,' sang what sounded like a very prissy young man. 'Ministry of Trade, can I help you?

'I'd like to speak to Mr Farnol, please.'

'Hang on one moment, I'll connect you.' The accent was ridiculous. You felt that he might break into song at any minute. The speech synthesizers who had programmed this reception machine obviously had a weird sense of humour.

'Department 9B East,' said another voice, softly modulated and female. 'Who do you wish to speak to?'

'Mr Farnol, please.'

There was a slight pause.

'Who is that speaking, please?'

'Jake, Jake Delagard. I'm his son.'

'Well, I'm afraid he's not come in today, Jake.'

He suddenly remembered that his mother had said that his dad was going off on one of his trips.

'When will he be back, do you know?' They must at least know approximately how long his trips would last.

'I'm afraid we don't know. Someone phoned to say he had flu.' The voice sounded extremely sceptical and a little frustrated. 'It might well be a week before he comes in. Can I help you?'

'No, no thank you. I'll try his home.'

'Can I reroute you?'

'No, no thank you.' The voice might well belong to a real person. There was no way of telling these days. If his dad was shamming flu again the last thing he'd want was his son drawing attention to the fact, someone trying to contact him.

His father's wristcom was turned off – par for the course if he was trying to avoid work. The phone at his flat merely chirruped away unanswered. Jake had thought the tale of the flu was suspicious anyway. His dad was prone to 'fall ill' when the baseball League was on or when anything else occurred that he fancied rather than work. But at the moment there were no league matches so where was he?

He had sent him this card. Why had he not mentioned it last night when he phoned? He suddenly remembered his mother's white face and distracted air, the cut hand trembling under his.

His unease sharpened into worry. Something had happened to his dad, something his mother couldn't or wouldn't tell him, something, he suddenly thought, to do with Runa Seven. His mother was always unhappy about going there. As far as he could tell every administration Runa Seven had ever had had been corrupt and his father was always complaining about them when he had to deal with them.

He tried the card again using his dad's private home password. The machine became positively genteel.

'I am sorry to inform you that on the next wrong password following this message the program will self destruct.'

He shoved the card into his shirt top pocket. He needed Stick Michaelis. Here was a card which would tell him what was wrong if only he could get into it. His mother would not have arrived in Runa Seven yet so it was too early to try and contact her. He would see Stick at the Ecoscience lecture in the afternoon. He would just have to contain his impatience and worry until then.

Chapter 4

There was a cheerful hubbub in the amphitheatre. Jake looked carefully for Stick but could not see him, feeling his heart sink as his eyes scoured the room. Undoubtedly he had not come. Stick came to the ERC when it suited him and not otherwise. Allie was there on the other side of the lecture hall holding court to a bunch of young students. She was standing in her usual position, head thrown back, accepting the youthful worship quite unconsciously and without conceit, laughing delightedly at somebody's joke, making him suddenly frantically jealous. She was a doctor's daughter – her mother was head of the micro-surgery unit at Kington Infirmary – and as such she would be one of the world's leaders. She knew her power and revelled in it.

'Get lost Snowy,' he said to a pimply youth, elbowing him aside.

Allie smiled at Snowy cheerfully, promising to catch him later, as he disappeared into the crowd and Jake felt again the rush of jealousy which turned his stomach.

'Allie, I've got to talk to you,' he said, hearing, at the same time the doors bang back to the central stage. 'It's urgent. After the lecture, OK?'

'OK,' said Allie, totally unfazed. 'C'mon, let's grab a seat before the herd arrives.' She settled her long slim shape comfortably into the seat, trainers balanced before her on the shoe bars running along the top back of the seats in front. 'Look, he's here already. It's the same one. Goody.'

It was indeed the same young lecturer from Ecopro that they had had before and now Jake didn't know whether to be pleased, since he was such a good lecturer, or fed up since Allie so patently approved of him. He was rather too good looking in a fair sort of way, the shock of blond spiky hair that fell over his forehead now tossed back as he surveyed the lecture theatre. A small thin woman seated behind him and to one side, half in the shadow frowned slightly.

He grinned engagingly and the perceptual maximiser allowed you to see the rather disarming slightly crossed left eye tooth and the crinkles of laughter around the eyes.

'I'll show you the film first. That should shut you all up and let you get settled down and then I'll do the demonstrations. Last time we talked about the Love Canal Syndrome, the poisoning of the soil: this time we're looking at problems with the ozone layer. My name's Sandy by the way, for those of you who've just made it for the first time, Sandy Stewart, from

Ecoproguardia – exaggerated pause – known and loved by you all as Ecopro.'

A few of the girls wolf whistled and Sandy's smile became even broader. The lights dimmed and the lecture was started.

Even though Jake was fascinated by the subject he found he could not concentrate – there was always the little niggle at the back of his mind about his dad. Under normal circumstances he would have been absorbed – he wanted to do something like this for a career himself. Of course, his mother had had his name down for a job at the Ministry of Trade since before he was born but once given the post, assuming he qualified, he could always transfer later on.

He tried to make a serious effort to listen.

'Ecoproguardia has been given the prestigious Central Administration contracts to oversee the research programs in all the Green Enclaves in the Runas where such Enclaves are possible,' said the voice, as the film walked you between wonderful trees, light dappling through the leaves and checkering the grass below in golds and greens and blacks.

'We have been given the job of restoring the land which our forefathers ruined. This is no easy task.' The film climbed through the shifting green light to the tree tops, panned across the waving green sea of the Enclave and showed them, immediately beyond its borders, the yellow, dried out ground of the world outside, the only world which they knew, the world of the yellow weed.

'For every success there are a hundred failures,' the voice continued, 'And years of painstaking effort are needed to eradicate the poisons which our forefathers gifted to us. They bear a terrible responsibility for the damage done to our planet. Initially they may not have known what they were doing, but later,' the voice deepened in accusation, 'they knew only too well.'

Yes, yes. They knew all that. The trouble dated from the time of the Blind Ages – nothing much to start with and most people knew nothing about it. When they had first discovered that the ozone was thinning above the poles they had thought that it would reconstitute itself without difficulty and then later had tried draconian measures to halt the damage. They had not worked. And then came the diseases, the skin cancers, animals and people suffering from acute conjunctivitis, a herd of cattle in the Andes gone blind and wandering to their deaths over the mountain edge, a growing variety of immune deficiency diseases, of which Aids was but one and finally the great plague, which had killed a third of the world's population before it was stopped.

And then the planet itself had begun to die. Firstly the oceans died. The plankton first, killed by the huge doses of ultra violet light no longer diffused by an ozone layer virtually destroyed. Then the land, crop yields falling, seeds finally refusing to germinate at all, leaving only the dreadful mustard coloured weed, one of the few growing things apparently impervious to the new light. Everybody had assumed that whatever else happened food would always grow. They had not foreseen the effect of the light and the chemical imbalance on the chlorophyll, altering it by some hideous alchemy so that everything grew thin and pale and etiolated and lacking all goodness. Everything to eat now had to be grown under specially tinted glass.

And of course, as the sea and all green things had died, so the earth had begun to suffocate from the lack of the oxygen which they had supplied. No wonder the nature religions threatened destruction and the end of the world. Now it was the oxygen pack drip feeding to his arm through the little artificial lung and the visors and the creams.

The lights came up and Sandy began to outline the types of research which his department undertook: largely genetic engineering of various kinds to increase the stock of the most resistant plants. He made one or two excellent jokes at the expense of the ERC's Director who kept two rather stunted spider plants in her office. Jake began to stop worrying about the card.

'We also analyse how to best obtain substances from plants which might be needed in the field of medicine, or how they might be reproduced synthetically and soil analysis to provide the best possible growing conditions for such plants.

The woman sitting behind Sandy looked out over the audience and Jake suddenly had the odd feeling that she was watching Sandy carefully. Sandy's voice had taken on an unaccustomed seriousness. 'I will not minimise to you, the next generation, the problems which face you. We have not managed, as yet, to replicate the success of the mustard weed. It is still the only species which can survive unaided outside the shields which we use for the Enclaves or without the tinted glass. Any living thing so far lives in despite of world conditions. Only by making sure that these conditions improve can we help your children to survive.'

No wonder they were so anxious for the green Enclaves to survive, Jake thought, the thin poor atmosphere struggling to regenerate itself. And now all this bad news about the Enclaves in Runa Seven.

Sandy clearly loved his work. He spoke with real passion and feeling.

'The ozone is being replenished,' he was saying, 'if painfully slowly. And we have recently discovered a plant which, I think, may reproduce quickly outside and will speed up that process. I think Ecopro may be onto something.' The bright blue eyes sparkled with enthusiasm.

Ecopro, his mother had told him, spent immense sums on research and development and had a high success rate in reclaiming land. Some experimental deserts were now, apparently, flourishing holiday clubs for the superrich and in parts of the Sahara you could actually go without oxygen. Em had joined one of their kiddie's clubs and had been given all sorts of goodies and a Save the Earth badge.

Sandy was demonstrating how the force fields above the Enclaves were held in place. 'Of course,' he was saying, 'It represents a tremendous cost in terms of generated power, and where possible we are replacing them with particle dispersers, but it's worth it.' The impish grin appeared again. 'And you can actually get to see some of the work yourselves. Ecopro has organised a sort of open day. It's very rare since the Enclave is basically a sterile area and that means that usually no one is allowed in. However, we are permitted to set up educational visits for the ERC's and your Centre has been chosen this year.

Now who are to be the lucky ones? We can only let in a very restricted number. Ms Kurosaka will let you know.'

Sandy turned to the woman who had been seated behind him on the platform and you suddenly realised where the power lay. The calm unsmiling face of a Runa Three representative surveyed the hall.

'We have consulted with the school authorities...' she had a little trouble pronouncing her 'r's', 'And all those with an Alpha in ecoscience can come. Of course, if you're not interested then your place can go to someone who is, so we would be grateful if all Alphas who intend going would register as well. After the Alphas there are a few places remaining. Since so many thousands of students use one Resource Centre and only a small group can be offered an opportunity to visit the Station we will use the school random selector system to choose those who can go and the resulting names will be vetted by staff.'

She looked out over the audience, her pale golden skin and black hair shining in the overhead lighting. 'Please put your names down now and then come back at six this evening to find out if you have been chosen. You will then have to return tomorrow for your security clearance.' She smiled distantly. 'Good luck.'

Jake went to put his name down and, while standing in the queue, chatted to Sandy who was pouring himself a coffee from the dispenser at the side of the registration desk.

'That was a brilliant explanation of how the power shields work,' he said. 'And I wanted to ask if there was anything which people outside the Enclaves could do to assist the research.'

'Come and work for us,' said Sandy jokingly. 'We always need more good scientists. What subjects are you taking at the moment?'

'I'd love to,' said Jake, he told him what he was studying and they chatted for a few moments more until he was able to register his name with the secretary at the front. He was dimly aware that the woman was watching them both and when he had turned to leave her eyes pursued him thoughtfully out of the room.

'Phone your mum straight away,' said Allie practically when he had told her all about it. 'She'll tell you if there really is anything amiss.'

He had to find a holocom that worked since his wristcom did not have the required range to phone Runa Seven and he had to use nearly all his bribe money to buy a paycard. Once he had got through the man at the desk said, after he had tried an internal number, 'Mrs Delagard is in conference. Who is speaking please? Is it urgent? I can fetch her if you like.'

'No, it's not important,' he said. 'I'll try later.'

He felt frustrated and the anxiety began to spread inside him.

'Look,' he said to Allie. 'I'll go to Stick's and get him to tell me what's on the card and then I'll go to my father's place. Perhaps he'll be back by then. Do you want to come with me to Stick's?'

Allie frowned. 'I'm sorry, I wish I could, but I've got a science tutorial which I mustn't miss. I could meet you at your father's place later on, if you like.' She grinned. 'I'm a computer bonzo, anyway, so I wouldn't be much use.'

They made arrangements to meet at Harry's and he got Stick's number from one of his friends. Stick's voice was cold and suspicious.

'Who's that?'

'Stick, it's Jake ...Jake Delagard here. Can I come and see you?'

'Jake Delagard? Oh yes, I know. Why? What do you want?' The voice was distinctly unwelcoming.

'I've got a job for you.'

'Computer job?

'Yes.'

There was a slight pause. 'OK. Know how to get here?'

'I'll find it,' said Jake firmly.

Stick rang off.

Chapter 5

There was at least a security corridor leading to Stick's place although no lightrail. While not being Stater territory it was definitely the wrong side of town. Jake caught a lightbus with a guard which took him most of the way down the corridor but then had to walk the last half mile or so along the corridor footpath.

Keeping well inside the corridor walls he trudged past a couple of the guarded exits where police units verified identity cards, until he could see, thankfully, the high rise appartments where Stick lived. As he checked out of the security corridor he felt, suddenly, terribly exposed, seeing, in front of him, the bare roadway leading past the appartments. It was an odd feeling as you went out of the gates, knowing that out here was the province of vandals, thieves and murderers, that only the security corridors were policed, that only they were safe.

One or two people scurried past him, probably just as frightened as he was, he thought. He ran as quickly as he could to the entrance way of Stick's tower.

There was no automatic guard, no voice recognition or palmprint procedure and when he spoke into the intercom an old man behind a steel grill pressed a button to open the door.

'Go on up,' he said, as Jake flashed his identity card at him. 'Stick told me you were coming.' Then he grinned happily, showing blackened and stained teeth. 'The lift's out of order, of course. But for you young things that isn't a problem, is it?'

His cackles pursued Jake into the stairwell. Stick lived on the fourteenth floor and Jake was mentally cursing the old man as he turned the corner onto Stick's landing, breathing heavily and with a slight pain in his side from having run the whole fourteen flights.

A large jolly girl opened the door and yelled, 'Stick it's one of your mates,' as she looked him over goodnaturedly. 'My, you're out over the wrong side of town, aren't you?'

He smiled weakly.

She had pink hair, an extremely tight jump suit and the sexiest way of walking that Jake had ever seen, as he trailed behind her through to Stick's bedroom.

She threw wide the door, yelling, 'He's here,' and stood back, allowing him just enough room to squeeze past her. He found that he was sweating slightly and he mumbled 'Thanks,' as she gave him, chuckling, a hefty nudge.

'Come and see me when you've finished here,' she said, 'I'm down the end of the corridor,' chuckled again and left him standing in the doorway.

The room was a disaster area. Spools of printer paper lay around in heaps, between and on pillows and sheets and bedcovers, none of which looked very clean. Computer cards and cables littered every flat surface. There were pieces of equipment on tables, on chairs, stacked on top of each other, standing on bookcases and screwed to the wall, expensive hifi equipment next to game machines, printers and servers, and in the centre of the room a huge desk, also piled with equipment, behind which was hunched a figure, his fingers floating over a screen.

It was easy to see where his nickname came from. Even seated at the desk he was clearly tall and skeletally thin. Red, frizzy hair fell across a white forehead in a tangled bush and he sucked his bottom lip with slightly crossed front teeth as he frowned at the screen. Then he looked up. Pale blue eyes assessed Jake, cold and lacking any interest.

'Yes?' he said.

'Stick, I need your help,' Jake said. He felt suddenly worried. The contempt in Stick's eyes was only too plain. It was well known that Stick wouldn't help some people if he didn't like them, no matter how much he was offered. And he knew that Stick despised the condo dwellers, people who profited from the poor, so he said, who let the rest go hang, who shut themselves up in their secure little towers and let everybody on the outside rot.

It wasn't like that, thought Jake despairingly, seeing the look in Stick's eyes.

'Why should I help little goody two shoes?' The voice was a sneer.

Jake's carefully prepared speech failed. 'Because you're the only one who can,' he said baldly.

The voice was still sardonic. 'Flattery will get you everywhere. Did we foul up our homework then?'

'No,' said Jake, 'No, it's nothing like that.' He held out the lesson card. 'I need you to get into this for me.'

Stick got up. Unfolding himself from the desk, a movement which most people would have accomplished in one go, was a whole series of operations involving each joint separately, knees, elbows, shoulders appearing suddenly at odd angles and in odd places, until finally he was standing in front of Jake. He stretched out his hand.

'Money,' he said. 'Money is all I need.'

How could he have been so stupid, thought Jake. He knew that Stick always demanded money and he had used anything of any value he had had on the phone call to Runa Seven. 'I haven't got any,' he said rapidly, 'but there's my card.'

'No cards,' said Stick. Plastic's traceable.'

'I'll get you some.'

Stick began to reseat himself. 'Come back tomorrow,' he said, 'and bring it with you.'

'I need it now,' he pleaded, knowing it wasn't going to work.

'Tomorrow,' said Stick implacably. 'Money or jewellery.'

'Please,' said Jake, 'it's urgent. I need it now. It's a matter of life and death.'

Stick looked at him in amazement. 'Do you think I was born yesterday?'

'It's true.' Jake was desperate.

'You can give me your watch, then.'

It was a present from Harry, really the only thing that his father and he had chosen together. It was an old-fashioned chronometer with mechanical workings. Fiendishly expensive. He'd wondered where Harry had got the money from.

'OK,' he said.

Stick took the card and slid it into the machine, saying, 'Game you want to pinch, is it?'

'No,' said Jake. He hesitated a moment. How much should he tell Stick? He looked at the blank screen, saw the small symbol flash and then read the words again. The machine said courteously, 'Please log in,' waited for five seconds and then went blank.

'Something's happened to my dad,' he said. 'I don't know what.'

But Stick wasn't interested. He was looking at the blank screen while fishing in a box beside him for another card which he waved at Jake, grinning cynically. 'The hacker's friend,' he said, sliding it into one of the fifteen drives in the stack. 'Your card's on a lockup. There are eighty four different sorts of lockup. For high security you can get three different ones at the very beginning but if you get past them you're OK. The friend will get me into the operating system.'

The jumble of characters on the screen meant very little to Jake. This could clearly take all day.

'You didn't come to the lecture.' he said, more for something to say than to ask why Stick had not shown up. Stick was talking to the computer, totally absorbed, filling the screen with characters and as suddenly removing them.

'Those jerks,' he said suddenly, bringing up a further jumble and swearing softly under his breath. 'Those jerks, prosing on about ecology and protecting the environment. You don't suppose for a minute that those big companies are in it for anything but the money, do you?'

Jake thought of the keen, idealistic, young man and was going to protest when he thought better of it. Better not to disagree with Stick at this point. The screen went blank again.

'They've usually got it on timers,' Stick said cheerfully. 'They put it in the V.B.L – that's a vertical blank to you,' he added, correctly interpreting Jake's puzzled look. 'It's a subroutine that scans the screen from top to bottom every fiftieth of a second. Put a 'divide by zero' error in the V.B.L and it'll lock the system up for years if you don't disable it.' The mouse ran and characters came and went.

'Obviously their security is very strict. Not like, say, Sopotos,' Stick smiled secretively. Sopotos was a large department store in uptown Kington. It stocked everything from washing machines to exotic pets and most people ordered and paid over the internet, although it was still possible to actually go and look round the store.

'These people are serious,' he said. 'They've got triple encryption and a Sandblaster. There's probably a second timer which'll stop access to any keyboard or voice recognition system, as well.'

Heaven knows what a Sandblaster is, thought Jake.

Suddenly the screen went blank again and the voice said, 'You have failed to give the correct password. Card now erasing.'

The machine clicked gear and the small red light came on. Stick banged a variety of keys on an old-fashioned keyboard but the little red light stayed on.

Jake looked at it in horror.

'Can't you stop it?' he said frantically – and then realised that it was too late. The red light had gone out.

He felt sick. The one clue that he had had as to what had happened to his father had been erased. He must have needed some kind of help and now he didn't know what to do because the message had gone.

Stick was still banging the keys. What did that help, thought Jake miserably. The card was dead.

'It's still in the machine memory,' said Stick cheerfully. 'So if you can't get in at the front door you just have to go in at the back.'

He hummed tunelessly for a bit. 'Can you think of any word which might be in this thing? If I know one word I can get the machine to look for it. Then it'll show me the compacted version from which we might be able to get the code.'

'I've no idea really,' Jake said. 'Try Stanford Farnol.' His father's name.

'Not there,' Stick said after a few minutes. 'I'll just have to try the random route.'

Another half an hour went by. Stick kept bringing up the jumble and sending it back but nothing seemed to work, no magic text appeared and it was clear that the message was gone for good.

He suddenly said aggrievedly, 'If this was so bloody important why didn't your dad send you the password?' but he didn't bother to listen to Jake's explanation. More time passed and he became more and more silent.

Then, very slowly, he began the intricate process of unfolding himself from the desk. Jake, looking at the foreign hieroglyphs still on the screen was sick at heart. That was it then. There was no way that he would know what his father's message was.

Stick was saying to him, 'The watch then,' and he was about to dispute tiredly, to say that Stick hadn't earned it, when suddenly the jumble converted into wonderful script and it began to scroll through lines of text and figures. It stopped scrolling as suddenly, reverted to the first page and sat there waiting for him to read.

He tore the watch from his wrist and gave it to Stick without looking at him, sitting in front of the monitor and instructing it to scroll again.

He did not understand. It was not a message at all. It was a list of figures with the odd bit of text and a photograph or two. At first he thought it must be a maths lesson but soon realised that it was part of a company report, a balance sheet with lists of costs and revenue for one of their products, some pictures, nothing else. There were about sixteen pages.

He scrolled through again frantically looking for the all important message from his father but there was nothing. It was a report for the product Aziproan.

He could have wept with frustration.

Why had his dad gone to the trouble to send him a card he couldn't read? And even if he could had no means of making use of? Why should such information be worth hiding under triple encryption? Aziproan was a reputable and much used medical product. The report would be available from the central disk library, or in a cloud store somewhere.

It made no sense. He felt a deep, pervading sense of disappointment.

Stick was watching him curiously, tightening the watch strap on his wrist.

Eventually he said, 'Not what you expected, eh?'

'No,' said Jake despairingly. 'No, I thought it was a message from my dad.'

And suddenly he found himself telling Stick all about it, all about the strange phone call and his mother's upset, Harry's letter and the card and now this.

'I don't even know who makes Aziproan or what it's supposed to be good for,' he finished miserably.

'Hang on a moment,' said Stick, leaving him and going out into the corridor. He could hear him in the bathroom opposite, rummaging in a bathroom cabinet.

'Ecopro,' he said triumphantly coming back waving a small phial in his hand. 'Me Mum has to have it. It's some sort of lung treatment. Very good. Fiendishly expensive, but she gets it on one of their Help programs.'

Jake suddenly remembered a half forgotten conversation with his mother about her job in Runa Seven and that she would be working with Ecopro. But why would Harry send him the company's accounts? Not even all of them, just the section dealing with Aziproan, a new wonder drug.

'Why send me this? You can read this in their company reports?'

'Unless,' said Stick slowly, 'your father knows what's wrong with this report. Suppose someone in the company is ripping them off – oh I don't know, cheating, embezzling in some way and somehow this report reveals it. Maybe the person was scared he would report them to Ecopro and has kidnapped him.'

'I can't see what good that would serve,' said Jake slowly. He began to have a bad feeling in his gut. What if it was his father who had been doing the embezzling and had now asked his mother to get him out of it?

'Or perhaps it shows a tax fiddle,' said Stick

'What do you mean?'

'Well, some firms have two sets of accounts, their own which tell them what's really going on and then the ones they show the tax office.'

'My father doesn't work in a tax office. He works in a boring bit of the Ministry of Trade. So does my mum for that matter. She was his boss for years.'

'What does he do?'

'Oh I don't really know,' said Jake tiredly. 'He checks that people keep to their quotas of imports and exports of certain substances.'

'Like what?'

'Well like titanium, for instance. There's only a tiny bit of it left. People are only allowed to use it in micro quantities.'

Stick knew this. It was the reason for the great machines, the rubbish eaters which, like whales taking in masses of krill and spitting out what was not needed, consumed huge mounds of rubbish and kept back the precious vital elements to be recycled constantly.

'Some of the poorer countries turn a blind eye to people using too much of a certain substance. Their Regional Administrations figure that they are so poor that they're entitled to use what they've got and don't see that they should stick to any sort of quota. But of course, everything companies make has to be listed and if it's discovered that they've used more of a substance than they're allowed then the company is fined.'

'It says here,' said Stick reading the report, 'that they make Aziproan in Runa Seven.'

The bad feeling in his gut increased. His mother was in Runa Seven. And she was working with Ecopro. Runa Seven didn't have a good track record when it came to checking on limited substances. Ecopro had had terrible problems there. He remembered reading something about the high number of cases of suicide and accident amongst their workers in Runa Seven; one lab technician had finished up with a scrambled brain. It was assumed his oxygen pack had failed. Ecopro had blamed Runa Seven vociferously and had taken the matter to the World Court but had got nowhere. It was bizarre.

'How can we find out if there's something wrong with Aziproan? Would it be possible to find out from their computer?'

Stick shrugged. 'I doubt it, especially if this card is anything to go by. Although, mark you, I now have some of the codes. It would be easier if I had access to one of their terminals. With this card I can undoubtedly get into their system.'

As if in line with their thoughts Stick's computer suddenly whistled loudly.

Chapter 6

The whistle brought Stick's eyes to gleaming life. 'Sopotos,' he said.

He ran to the computer saying, 'I had a bit of luck. I cracked Sopotos' code.' The pale blue eyes crackled with the old contempt. 'Their accounts are most revealing.' He grinned nastily at Jake, saying, 'you'd be amazed at who buys what and for whom.'

Jake stood by the machine and watched as columns and columns of accounts flashed by.

'That's it. See it.'

An account number had been highlighted and was flashing.

'It's old Ashrafi's account. Let's see what he's bought today. You'd be amazed at what he gets. All this lacy underwear. He's a really dirty old man. We'll just do a bit of quick transfer here.'

Jake watched as Stick hastily deleted some numbers and inserted others, thinking about Ashrafi, one of the town's most prominent lawyers, one of the upper class families who had come centuries ago from the Asian subcontinent and who now owned most of the country. He had seen him once on television and thought that he seemed an amiable old buffer.

'The stupid yonk doesn't know that he hasn't paid his bill for three months. He can't even check it. What it must be to have so much money you don't know what to do with it – and Sopotos will give him as much credit as he likes.' Stick was typing rows of numbers rapidly. 'Still, I daresay he'd be delighted to know he's helping the lower classes.'

Jake knew that minor theft of this kind was a game played by almost all hackers. It usually only involved trivial amounts since account numbers were changed on a regular basis and any large orders were checked at source but even so he felt annoyed.

In what way was Stick any different from the Stater on the train?

'Aren't you worried they'll catch you?'

'Nah. Let's take a troll along the hi-fi section shall we.' Stick whistled softly to himself as he called up the store display and ran up and down the aisles saying, 'I'll have that one and that and that,' tapping in the code for each item. Jake now saw where all the expensive equipment in Stick's room came from.

'The amounts are too small to call out the CFO's for, anyway. I only once made a real killing and that was a chap on the block who died if you'll pardon the pun. I used his account for ages before they discovered he'd popped his clogs and couldn't pay.'

He changed departments to the clothing section and stopped in front of a brilliantly coloured knitted scarf and leaned back to admire it.

Oh isn't that pretty! I'll send it to old Bill at the bottom of the stairwell. He had a terrible cold last week.' He tapped in a new code and a different address and then smiled contentedly.

'Each week I "open" a different account with a company whose code I've cracked, provide a false address etc, and if I'm lucky, like with Sopotos or whatever, I transfer the money to a new bank account I've opened also in a false name with instructions to send it on to me at my real account. Tomorrow, once Sopotos has done the order I'll put Ashrafi's address back in. Amongst all the orders they send out they won't know they didn't send it to him and he'll be wondering why nothing's come. It'll take ages. I close the false accounts and delete all reference to them only it will have transferred the money to me and Sopotos will send me some goodies in the interim. Neat, eh?'

'Robin Hood indeed' said Jake sourly.

'Unfortunately I can't use him again. Might get old Bill into trouble if they manage to trace it.'

'Not Robin Hood with a conscience surely?' said Jake.

Stick smiled the cynical smile and then leaned back in his chair, tilted his head back and clasped his hands behind his neck, closing his eyes. His skin was pale and the eyelids looked almost transparent. In this position he looked more angular and ungainly than ever.

'Now let's have a little think about your problem.'

'It's all right,' said Jake hastily. I'm going to Ecopro on the school trip in a couple of day's time and I'll maybe be able to find out something then.' The last thing he wanted was Stick Michaelis getting mixed up in his father's troubles. 'In the meantime I'll check out this report. They must be available from central company register I should think.'

'Do you want a hand?'

'Oh, I'll be all right.' Now he knew what the card said he was anxious only to get away from Stick's unsettling influence. And it was almost time for him to meet Allie at Harry's place.

Stick said, 'I'll come with you to Ecopro, if you like.'

The rejection rose promptly to his lips. He didn't want Stick with his pale blue eyes and his condemnation. He opened his mouth to say no and then thought, 'I'll need him if there's a computer.'

Stick was suddenly withdrawing.

'All right, all right, go on your own.'

It was true he needed Stick.

'No, please,' he said. It cost him to say it. 'I need you.' It was the best he could manage. 'But I don't see how you can get in.'

'Why's that?'

'Because you have to be either an Alpha or 'one of the chosen'.

Stick looked amused. 'If it's the school's random selector then it's no problem. Watch this.'

He slid another card into a drive and pressed a button, punching the school's number into a handset.

The terminal ran a series of menus until in a matter of seconds Stick was typing in his own name.

'Look at that, ' he said to Jake, 'How helpful. Fancy them picking little old me. It looks as if I'll be coming with you.' He smiled his world weary smile. 'A mindless idiot could get into the school computer.'

Allie was waiting at the prearranged spot and they all went up to his father's unit together. Jake sensed that something was wrong even as he was holding his palm over the recognition slot at the entrance.

'Oh my,' said Stick, surveying the wreckage, 'Somebody booked the wrong interior decorator.'

Jake and Allie said nothing, too stunned by the devastation to comment. Somebody had been there before them. Lamps, chairs and tables had been overturned and drawers wrenched out and their contents scattered; cupboard doors hung drunkenly from twisted hinges; books, papers, magazines, discs were lying about everywhere. A couple of cups were balanced precariously on the top of a chair back.

'Odd,' said Stick.

'Yes, very,' said Jake.

'No, I don't mean that,' said Stick following his gaze. 'Look around. Hifi, video, terminals....,' he was ticking things off on his long bony fingers, 'holocom ... new model, VR headset ...' he pointed at the floor, 'silver backed hairbrush, and probably any other bits and bobs of value – all here.'

'So it's not theft.' Allie said. 'They were looking for something.'

Jake headed for the kitchen. He knew exactly where his father kept anything of value. In the bottom of his steamer. The water container was a fixed unit in the bottom and only rarely needed to be taken out. Even more rarely as Harry usually never cooked. If you looked in it just appeared as if the holes were let into the base and sides of the steamer section with an outside indicator as to whether the water needed replenishing. But the water unit did indeed come out. And there was what they – whoever they were – had been looking for. There were two envelopes in the bottom of the steamer.

The first contained a photograph of a tree, and a standard analysis report from the Food and Nutrition section of the Ministry of Trade. He had seen the photograph somewhere before. The report from the Ministry of Trade contained a chemical breakdown of a sample of the breakfast cereal called Wheatie Pie.

Harry had highlighted one of the ingredients, c1507.4, and then doodled in the margin. It looked like the letters five and eight. The second envelope contained a bank statement and 180,000 Runa dollars, the equivalent of half a million old pounds. Although most Runas, the Regional United Nations Administrative areas, kept their own currency, there were also the pan-continental Runa dollars valid anywhere.

The sick feeling in his gut increased. Where had his father obtained such huge amounts of cash?

He left the cash in the steamer but took the photograph and the papers through to the living room where Allie was picking up papers from the floor.

'Are you fetching the police?' she said. 'Perhaps I shouldn't touch anything.'

'No,' he said wretchedly. 'No I can't.' He saw that he would have to explain.

'I think,' he said slowly, formulating his ideas as quickly as he could, 'that Harry might have got himself mixed up in something illegal ....Not serious,' he added quickly, seeing Allie's face, 'He wouldn't do anything to harm anyone and anyway...... anyway, it's possible that he wants to get out of it, whatever it is. I think it's something to do with Ecopro and Runa Seven. Look.'

He showed them the photograph and the formula.

Stick squinted at the photograph. 'Same tree in the photograph in that report,' he said 'Only, this one's got some background. Can you see the box with NE Enclave on it?'

Jake was still looking at the formula. 'I can't see what Wheatie Pie's got to do with it though. Perhaps that's something else. And I think he may have been accepting money to cover things up.'

Stick was unworried. People who accepted money, however come by, had his blessing.

'Well I don't suppose you could run an illegal traffic in Wheatie Pie. You obviously can't turn him in. Maybe he's hiding out somewhere until the fuss dies down. He just sent the report to you. Maybe he thought your mum would get it and be able to spoil whoever-it-is's little game without anyone knowing where the information came from.'

Allie was perturbed. 'It's beginning to look dangerous, Jake. Look at this place. I think you should go to the police.'

'I can't, can I?' he said. 'I might get him into trouble if I do. I'll have to ask my mother. What I'll do, I'll stay here. Then if Harry turns up I'll know straight away. Can I tell Margie I'm staying with you, Allie?'

'No problem. I'll prime my mother so that she says all the right things if Margie calls.'

'I can phone my mother from here and tell her.'

He plugged the holocom back in and found it still worked and the others tactfully left him and went off to the kitchen to see if anything remained in the fridge to eat. Soon he could hear Allie's sunny peals of laughter at the fridge's contents. He got through without any bother and was connected to his mother straight away.

She still looked neat and efficient, seated at the desk, looking straight into the camera. The holocom zoomed in in closeup. She looked tired and pale.

'Hi Mum,' he said. 'Have a good trip?'

'Yes thanks, Jake. Totally boring flight. So what's up? I'm sure you didn't phone me just to enquire about the trip?'

The problem with his mother, he thought, was that she was too smart by half.

'Mum,' he said, 'I tried phoning Harry.'

He saw the alarm and the anger start into her eyes.

'Don't talk to me about that man.' Her voice was a whiplash. 'And don't try and contact him. At least till I get back.' The small screen amplified the widening of her eyes with the shine of anger in them. Then she must have seen the look on his face for the anger died. 'I'm sorry, Jake, I've had enough of your father at the moment.'

'I thought he might perhaps be in trouble,' he said. 'He sent me a card but it's on a lockup. I thought perhaps I could scan it through to you now.' Once again he saw the alarm flicker in her eyes.

'No, don't do that.' There was a pause. 'Wait till I get back. I'll deal with it then.' She was obviously thinking swiftly, deciding how much she could confide to a public line and picking her words carefully. 'Look, Jake, you know I'll try and work everything out for the best. Definitely don't try to contact your father at the moment. Wait till I get back. OK?'

'OK,' he said reluctantly.

'If all goes well I might be back a couple of days early. I'll give you a ring tomorrow.'

'I'll be at Allie's for a day or two,' he said.

'That's fine. Sorry I can't stop now Jake, I've got a lot of work to get through. Look after yourself.' She smiled, 'Love you. Bye,' and she was gone.

He felt totally bereft. The others rejoined him and listened to his report.

'Your mum's not stupid,' said Allie. 'You'd better do as she says.'

'I suppose so,' he said reluctantly.

'I mean, it isn't as if you've got anything definite, is there? There's just this formula and the photograph. There might be any sort of explanation for those. It's true your Dad's been burgled but that happens all the time. It's not necessarily connected.'

'I suppose so.' He sighed.

'And it sounds as if, if there is anything wrong, it's in Runa Seven and your mum's there, so she's the best person to look after it. I'll check this formula out for you, if you like, and see if it tells us anything.'

'And,' she added, seeing his anxiety, 'We'll get to look around Ecopro's Research Unit in a day or so. We might be able to find out something there.'

'Let's just go and make sure we're on the list,' said Stick. 'I don't think there's much more we can do here, is there. Shall we go?'

Nobody noticed him sliding a piece of paper that had been lying amongst the clutter on the table into his pocket.

Chapter 7

They were a little late arriving at the lecture hall and most of the people who had been chosen had already been informed.

'Ah, it makes you want to puke, that random selector,' said one of girls pushing her way past. 'I haven't been picked once in all the years I've been at this ERC.'

Stick went to the front and checked that his name was on the list while Jake and Allie, who were automatically chosen being Alphas, went to join the group gathered round Sandy Stewart. He was packing away the last of his equipment, having just finished his final lecture. So many students attended an ERC that the lectures were repeated four or five times in the course of a day. He looked tired but cheerful and various students were asking him questions to which he was responding with unfailing good humour.

Jake watched him a little dejectedly. If there was anything wrong at Ecopro it seemed unlikely to be anything to do with Sandy. His mother's instructions still rang in his ears and he knew that really he ought not to pry any further. It was fairly obvious to him that his dad was involved in something shady and that his mother knew about it. He couldn't help feeling irritated though that she always seemed to keep his father at arm's length. He was his dad as well as her ex and he was entitled to some togetherness.

'Trust me to do what is for the best,' she had said. Perhaps he should just leave it at that.

There was nothing to stop him asking Sandy one or two things, though, was there, just out of curiosity? He pushed his way forward and as he got to the front circle Sandy saw him and smiled.

'Ah, our budding ecologist.'

'I just thought I'd ask,' said Jake. 'I understand that Ecopro contributes a lot to Help programs in the community. Do they supply the drugs freely or does the Administration contribute anything?'

Sandy looked interested. 'Certainly Ecopro does a lot of good work in the community, hand in hand with the Health Department, of course. And, as far as I know, all the drugs offered, that is, those which are actually made by Ecopro, are given freely. I must confess, though,' he smiled disarmingly, 'I don't know too much about that side of it as I only work at the research end.'

'Is Aziproan one of your products?'

'Yes, indeed,' said Sandy. 'We're very proud of it. It's one of the most significant breakthroughs in lung treatment that we've had in the last decade.'

There must be something about Aziproan thought Jake desperately. 'Is it true that they've recently found some problems with it?'

The puzzlement was genuine, the young face open and concerned. 'Not that I know of. As you may know it's highly successful in the treatment of lung and respiratory problems.'

'But quite expensive.'

You could see that Sandy did not know what he was getting at. 'Yes, but it's an 'authorised' product so most people can get it on prescription now. And quite a lot is sent out on our Help Programs totally for free.'

There must be something thought Jake. Why had his father sent him the card?

'May I ask what sort of progress is being made in Runa Seven?'

It was a shot in the dark. He had not really expected a response but saw, in that instant, the fear in the man's eyes, a faint stiffening to his face, and Sandy said quickly, too quickly, 'I'm afraid I know nothing about Runa Seven. Experimental work in other Runas is not my province.'

And then another question came from somewhere else in the crowd and the moment was gone.

Stick reappeared jauntily at his side, saying, 'All done and dusted. We come back tomorrow for our security clearance', and Allie was saying, 'I'm sorry Jake, I've got to dash now. Meeting my mother at seven. Come round tonight, if you'd rather. We'd love to have you.' She gave him the smile which caused his heart to fail within him. 'My mother fancies another game of chess with you since you beat her last time.' And then she too, was gone.

He phoned Margie to tell her he might stay over at Allie's. He used the wristcom but could imagine Margie sitting in front of the holocom phone talking to it. You couldn't train her to carry on doing what she was doing, carrying it about. She believed that you had to talk properly to the machine, even if no one could see you at the other end. Margie, in his opinion, was a stupid and selfish woman and would be delighted if he stayed away all week.

She made a few token protests at his not coming in. 'You might think of me a little bit,' she was saying, 'here all on my own with only Emma for company. I know it's a condo but you're not always safe, even here.'

She really was the dumbest female, thought Jake.

Her voice was still aggrieved. 'Don't sniff at me young man. For a start, somebody managed to get into the mail boxes just this morning and everybody's mail was scattered everywhere. But they don't seem to have taken anything.'

She laughed self-importantly and he imagined her pushing her hair back in that affected way she had.

'I'd already sent your mother's mail down to the secretary by courier, of course, and I told her what had happened and she seemed to think that everything was there all right. The condo committee said it must have been one of these activist groups or something. But it just shows. None of us is safe.'

He could see that it was the only bit of excitement which had occurred in her day. She spent her whole time parked in front of the television with a box of chocolates and a hanky for the soaps.

As he came into the main hallway a gang of youths rushed past him, larking about, playing tag, one of them shoving into him and knocking him back against the wall so that he half fell to the floor.

'Sorry mate,' said the young man, pulling him up and rubbing a mark off his jacket. 'Sorry. In a rush. Didn't look where I was going. Sorry.' He gave another brush to Jake's jacket.

'Don't worry,' said Jake, struggling to get his breath. 'I'll live.'

The lad smiled and was off.

A Centre guard came tearing up, as always too late. 'I say, are you all right?' he said.

He had, in fact, fallen on his elbow and it felt quite sore – the skin was probably scraped – but he said quickly, 'Oh I'm all right,' embarrassed to have fallen over in public.

'It was odd,' said the guard. 'You'd almost have thought that he was trying to knock you over.'

'It's OK,' said Jake again, patting his pocket. 'No harm done.' As he expected his wallet with the small amount of remaining bribe money, phone card and lesson cards had gone. It was stupid. Nobody carried any amount of cash any more, nothing really worth stealing. Only a small amount of bribe money in case of attack. The credit cards were so complicated it needed a massive operation to practice fraud. Even so, petty theft of this kind was very common. It was what made life so restrictive. You could never leave the security corridors, never go off somewhere, on your own, away from the crowds. You had to stay somewhere where it was safe. And then, even there, you were not safe.

And then he remembered his father's card. It was still tucked into his top shirt pocket.

They had been after the card. They had tried the mail box, not found it and somehow decided that he must have it.

He turned and ran back towards the amphitheatre, heading for the back entrance from which visiting lecturers usually left. Sandy and another young man were loading all the equipment into a small lightvan labelled Ecoproguardia, laughing and exchanging pleasantries. Ms Kurosaka came out and stood next to Sandy, waiting until the van had left and then beginning to talk to him earnestly. Her expression was serious and Jake, who had been going to talk to Sandy himself, decided to choose a more appropriate moment.

The young man appeared to be disputing and the woman's demeanour became more cold and imperious than ever; it looked as if she was laying the law down with a vengeance.

'You are the obvious person to go,' she was saying. 'You know the man. I admit it's an odd spot to choose but research is research.'

Sandy looked as if he would have protested again but Kurosaka had spun on her heel and was leaving. Jake stood back into the shadows behind the door and waited until she had disappeared from view. Sandy watched her retreating back, an expression of anger and, yes, thought Jake, fear on his face and then spun round himself and slipped back into the ERC, half running down the stairs to the lightrail.

Jake followed him, keeping at a safe distance, waiting for the opportune moment. A lightrail slid into the ERC station just as they arrived and Jake had to run to catch it, missing the carriage in which Sandy was travelling, and ending up in the one behind. He had no clear idea of what he wanted to ask him. Only that he had seemed an honest man and that he clearly knew more about Runa Seven than he was saying.

About three stops further on Sandy got out and Jake jumped out as well and ran to the end of the platform, catching him just as he was about to leave. 'Sandy,' he said, 'Sandy, can I talk to you a minute?'

The cheerful open smile had gone and a nervous, frightened young man stood in front of him.

'You're Jake, aren't you? Jake Delagard. Look son, I'm sorry I can't talk to you. It's more than my job's worth.'

'Why?' said Jake. 'Please. I just want a little information.'

'No,' he said firmly, 'I'm sorry. Please leave me alone.'

He looked up the platform, spun on his heel and headed out of the station onto a security corridor footpath and almost without thinking Jake followed. Sandy walked briskly and then, suddenly, turned off through one of the exits, flashing his ID at the policeman guarding the gate. On the far side of the exit he began to run.

Jake, held up by the policeman who wanted to know what he might want in an Estate when he lived in a condo beyond Crater Edge, realised that he would lose him. 'Look, it's my old aunt,' he said. 'She's lived here for years. She says she doesn't want to move.' He was amazed at how easy it was to lie.

The policeman didn't look convinced and so he added, 'That chap who's just gone through, Sandy Stewart, he'll vouch for me.'

'Oh OK,' said the policeman grumpily. 'But watch your step in there, they're either rogues or nutters the most of them.'

'Thanks,' said Jake. 'I won't be long.'

Sandy had run off to the right, along a side street between two large buildings and Jake ran as fast as he could into the street and looked down it desperately. At the far end, he could see someone disappearing around the next corner. His legs on automatic he sprinted off down the street hoping against hope that he wouldn't lose Sandy in the jungle of buildings that lay ahead of them.

Suddenly he knew he was in Stater territory. He almost fell over an old woman lying in the gutter hugging a carrier bag with the top of a bottle protruding from it. She was bundled up in a man's old fashioned overcoat fastened with string and as he swerved to avoid her she rolled over onto her side and began to crawl along the pavement, heading determinedly for a doorway. There was nobody else on the street at all, only the blond headed young man running away into the distance.

Close to the security corridor there had been larger detached houses with high walls and fences, but as he got further and further away the housing became more and more dilapidated, the fences which once had been electrified now mostly torn down, offering no protection. The naked fronts were dark, and silent, although here and there were small signs of life, pieces of dirty washing flapping in the breeze, a torn curtain blowing at an upstairs window.

He was running past a patch of waste ground. He felt terribly naked and exposed. Heaps of rubbish lay about on the waste land and in the street and the stench was stomach churning. The road was deeply pot holed, not like the skateboarding surfaces in a condo village where you could achieve a smooth glide with no effort.

Through the middle of the waste land were rolls of barbed wire so that it looked like a war zone from the days before the Blind Ages, even to the scabrous mustard coloured weed and the brown earth. An old railway track ran next to the road and beyond that were the rusting iron skeletons of burnt out warehouses. And to think that he had once thought it would be a treat to go beyond the confines of the safety walls, alarms and passwords of the condo villages.

The little clicks from his oxygen pack were increasing. Living near the Green Enclave you didn't notice the pack so much since the concentration of oxygen in the air was so much higher. Out here life must be more desperate. Oxygen was so expensive and it was precisely those who were too poor to buy it who needed it most.

Sandy was turning a corner ahead of him but he was gaining on him. He sprinted to the corner and stopped stunned. Sandy had disappeared.

He ran back and looked in the opposite direction. There was no sign of him. Then he saw the small door leading through an archway into a narrow alleyway. He pushed the door gently and it swung in.

The body was sprawled in an ungainly heap, just beyond the entrance to the courtyard. Jake ran across and knelt beside him, turning him over so that he could see who it was, knowing that it was Sandy.

'Sandy, Sandy, are you all right,' he said, feeling desperately for the young man's pulse. Sandy's head lolled back, he was unconscious but breathing heavily, the oxygen pack puffing and clicking rapidly as he dragged in each breath. Jake looked round to see if there was anyone who might help and had just had time to register that someone was behind him when the fingers fastened around his throat and he was pulled back away from the young man.

He tried a couple of manoeuvres from his karate class to break the person's hold on him but he had been caught off balance and the fingers were made of steel. Suddenly one hand left his throat and he realised that they were tearing at his oxygen pack, rending the delicate valve from its casing, unplugging the tubing, cutting off the vital, life-giving gas.

He tried again to break the hold on his throat but as he scrabbled at the fingers he found his strength sapping, his energy draining away and suddenly the effort was too much, a dark mist swirled in front of his eyes and he plunged into the black hole of unconsciousness.

Back in his bedroom Stick hummed idly as he propped the piece of paper on the computer terminal in front of him. It was really quite helpful having the bank statement, along with the little list of codes which had been on Harry's personal organiser lying in the living room. It was not often that he had all the information that was required. It would make this bit of hacking so much easier.

Chapter 8

Jake came to feeling violently sick and almost suffocating. It was dark in the room where he lay and as he stirred and moved his arm he realised that he was covered with something like sacking. Groaning, he attempted to sit up and as he moved something was clamped over his face and mouth.

He struggled violently and heard a voice, far off, saying, 'Breathe.'

He wrenched himself over to his side but was not strong enough to fight the retaining hands and fell back gasping. The sense of suffocation grew and as he struggled someone held the top of his head and clamped whatever it was to his face more firmly and said again, 'Breathe, stupid.'

He was too weak to fight and his lungs were desperate for air, dragging in a breath despite his efforts not to. Nothing happened and he continued to breathe, deeply and raggedly at first and then more regularly, his head gradually clearing and his eyes adjusting to the light in the room.

A small elfin face with huge dark eyes surrounded by a bush of tangled hair was looking down at him, saying, "You must have wriggled and knocked it off.'

He realised that it must be an old fashioned face mask that he was wearing, that someone behind him was lifting him and slipping the mask's retaining straps around his face and then laying his head back gently on the pillow.

'We found you,' she said. 'You were lucky, we must have got to you almost immediately.'

The young face disappeared and another leant forward over him, a terrible gargoyle-like apparition, with blotched parchment skin and a smile that revealed crooked and blackened teeth and wrinkled lips. The old woman cackled. 'See, I told you he'd be all right.'

'Maggie is brilliant,' said the little voice reverently.

'Just a few little tricks of the trade,' said the old woman complacently. 'At least there's no fracture to the skull.' She cackled again. 'Of course you'll have a headache. LIE DOWN.'

A bony finger prodded him in the chest and he collapsed back onto the pillow.

'Drink this.'

A hand lifted his mask momentarily so that he could sip from the cup that the old woman was offering him. It tasted of nothing very much and he had hardly begun to worry about where he was and what had happened to him when he fell asleep.

He was dragged back to consciousness several hours later by an insistent little voice. 'Come on,' it said, 'Wake up. More medicine.'

He felt as if he had been fighting something large and heavy. His head was leaden and his mouth full of ashes.

The little face was bent over him again and now that he was accustomed to the light he could see that it looked concerned. 'Come on. Maggie said you should have woken up by now.'

Once again hands held him and lifted him.

'I'm Ginny,' she said. 'I found you. Drink this.'

He lifted the mask and drank. It still tasted of nothing.

'Finish it. Maggie's good with herbs.' He could see that the little face was alive with curiosity and interest. 'What's your name?'

He wondered fleetingly if he should give his real name. 'Jake.' He tried to move his head to see who it was sitting behind him and winced as the hot wires in his neck pulled tight and stopped him dead.

'Don't worry movin', lad,' came the voice. 'My name's Robert. I carried you in.'

Ginny's eyes looked even larger and darker than he remembered them, the curiosity making them sparkle.

'What were you doing in our estate? Why were you fighting with that young man? Are you a condo dweller?'

'Yes,' he said answering the last question first since it was the easiest.

And then Robert was saying, 'Leave him be, lass, let him sleep some more,' was settling him comfortably back again onto his pallet and he dropped again into darkness.

The screaming of sirens awoke him the third time and the unmistakable roar of armoured cars sweeping into the courtyard. There were hurried steps on the stairs and urgent whisperings outside his door and then people were in the room, rough hands were gathering him up between them, carrying him out into an even greater darkness. He could smell the urgency and the fear.

In the flash of a torch he saw momentarily Ginny's face, anxious, alarmed, hearing her say, 'Quickly, quickly,' and then he was being hauled up a ladder into what he judged was a loft and dragged hastily across the floor. By the thin slats of light coming through the slanting ceiling he could just make out his handlers, the one at his head a short, square, sturdy young man with curly brown hair, the other just a shadowy image at his feet. On his right was Ginny.

'It's the police,' she said. 'Somebody must have tipped them off. We'll do our best not to let them get you.'

He was being lowered into a small hole through a trap door.

'Careful,' said Robert's voice, 'mind his head,' and a square capable brown hand appeared in the torch's beam, passing him down the mini oxygen flask. A length of sacking was thrown into his cubby hole with him, and the square of wood was lowered, entombing him once more in darkness. It sounded as if heavy objects, furniture, perhaps, to judge by the screech of squeaking castors, was being dragged over the top of his trapdoor and then the footsteps disappeared out of range. There was a further noise and someone said, 'Let them out, let them run about.' and then the soft grating of a trapdoor being lowered carefully and quietly into place and the silence growing.

He felt totally confused. What was happening? Why had Ginny said that they wouldn't let the police get him? Someone had attacked him as he bent over Sandy and had torn off his oxygen pack. Did the police think he had hurt Sandy? He saw again Ginny's troubled little face and heard Robert saying 'Mind his head now.' These people were obviously on his side.

He could hear small scratching noises above him, something skittering across the floor of the loft. He thought of the heavy furniture sitting on top of the trapdoor. He would never get out. He found that he was sweating and that the headache had returned in earnest. What was happening?

Far below he could hear a bell shrill and then the murmur of voices. Then feet, heavy, boot shod, official feet clumping up the stairs, across landings, into rooms, the sound of cupboard doors being opened and slammed shut, and finally a voice, almost below him saying, 'Is that the loft? You've been up there recently.'

It was an accusing statement, not a question.

A murmured reply.

The first voice raised in exasperation. 'You don't expect me to believe that, do you?'

More mumbled replies almost drowned by the skittering and scratching noises somewhere near him.

'Get the ladder.'

There was a loud thump and then the crash of the trapdoor dropping back, echoing even into his hiding hole and he could imagine the policeman at the top of the ladder with his head and shoulders poking into the loft.

'Bloody hell, look at them.' he said.

Now the trapdoor was open Jake could hear the response.

'I told you. I told you we'd got mice. I've just been up putting the poison down. It's in those little trays.'

There was an oath of disgust from the policeman. 'How you people can live like this I don't know.'

'You try keeping these places clean.' Robert's voice was surly.

'Don't put your hands near the trays.' warned the first voice. He recognized it as the old woman's. 'It's quite dangerous if you get it on your hands.'

Jake held his breath. The trapdoor slammed back down, and the sounds of the boot-shod feet receded.

It was hours later before they came to let him out.

'Sorry about that, lad,' said Robert. 'But better that than if they'd got you.'

Jake, sitting on the edge of his pallet bed again, with the family gathered round, looked up puzzled.

'How do you know they were looking for me?'

'Look,' said Ginny, thrusting an ancient type of tablet into his hand showing a collection of web news pages.

The first said that Sandy Stewart, a research scientist at the North Eastern Green Enclave had been found dead, stabbed, in the Fairfield Estate. A spokesman for Ecoproguardia, who ran the Research Unit, said that it was an absolutely terrible thing to have happened. Mr Stewart had been one of their brightest members of staff, a gifted lecturer who inspired young people with his own enthusiasm. He would be sorely missed. The police, the printout reported, were pursuing their inquiries.

'He was alive all right when we left,' said Ginny, 'because I checked. He was breathing all right, his oxygen pack was working OK, in fact he seemed to be coming round. We went back to help him as well once we'd got you inside but he'd gone.'

The next printout said that witnesses had come forward both at the lightrail terminus and within the Fairfield estate to report that Mr Stewart was last seen being pursued by a teenager in a blue anorak. The young man had spoken to a policeman on the security corridor gate. The description they gave fitted Jake exactly. The young man, it said, was perhaps the last person to have seen Mr Stewart alive, and should contact the police so that he could be eliminated from their enquiries.

'Eliminated from their enquiries, ha!' said Ginny.

The third printout said that witnesses had seen the young man threaten Mr Stewart with a knife at the lightrail terminus.

'You were on the main news as well,' said Robert.

Jake felt as if he understood nothing. 'So why didn't you hand me over to the police?'

Ginny's mother answered. She was a tall woman, tough, angular and harsh faced, as his mother might have been, he thought, had she been born into a Stater home instead of an Employed, Grade Two, family.

'There's no love lost between folks round here and the police. They've forgotten what it was like to have the hard times. In fact, they usually don't come into the estates at all.'

'We knew that the chap was alive when we left,' said Robert, 'He hadn't been stabbed when we saw him so it looked like you were being set up. Thought you might like a bit of time, like, to work out who might be doing it.'

Oh no, Jake thought. He hadn't even checked. He patted each of his pockets frantically and tried them all but it was just as he had suspected. The photograph and Harry's card had disappeared.

He felt suddenly totally bereft. If Allie had read the news printout what would she think? She would guess who had been pursuing Stewart. Had his mother been told?

'I don't know what's happening,' he said wretchedly. 'I think it's something to do with my dad.'

'You don't need to tell us if you don't want to. You can stay here as long as you like, as long as it's safe. The police won't come back in a hurry. It's like ma says, they don't usually venture into the estates. We have our own methods of sorting out them as tries cheating on their neighbours.'

Jake tried desperately to think clearly. He realised that he had quite lost track of time, that he did not know how long he had been unconscious, for how many hours he had been in this little room.

'How long is it since you found me?'

'We brought you in yesterday about seven o'clock,' said Ginny. 'It's twelve o'clock now.'

'Time I was making lunch,' said the mother, rising and looking down at him. 'You'll need something.'

A whole day! He scarcely noticed her leaving the room. He had been unconscious a whole day. He reared up on the pallet bed. 'I must go. I've got to get into the Green Enclave.'

Was it morning or afternoon that they were going to give out the security clearance tags? He struggled to remember.

'The Green Enclave?' said Robert. He noticed that Robert and Ginny were looking at each other oddly. 'What do you want to get in there for?'

'It's a school trip,' he said. 'We were supposed to get our security clearance tags today.

The tension in the atmosphere lessened.

'Well you can write that off,' said Robert. 'Right now. For a start, if you go out now the police will have you sure as eggs is eggs. And I'd want to know a lot more about what's going on before I let them get their hands on me.'

'But,' said Jake slowly, 'I think that the answer to my problems lies in the Enclave. Somehow it's got something to do with Ecopro.'

'Oh, aye,' said Robert. 'The chap who was killed comes from there.'

'But nobody gets into a Green Enclave, ever,' said Ginny.

'But I've got to try,' said Jake, trying to stand up on shaky legs. 'I think my dad must be in danger.'

But it was true, he thought, that nobody got into a Green Enclave. They were so precious that they had the most sophisticated types of guard systems to protect them, fully automated along the external fences, and then who knew what inside. The fence shields were so powerful that somebody caught by them would be knocked unconscious for up to a week, quite apart from the huge fine and the criminal listing on your identity card.

It was rumoured that the occasional poacher who actually got inside if a barrier was faulty was never quite right afterwards. The magnetic force from the ozone shields probably damaged you in some way. And it was also rumoured that the types of stun gun carried by the Enclave patrols were particularly vicious. Whichever way you looked at it, getting into an Enclave illegally was well nigh impossible.

Ginny pushed him firmly back. 'Don't be silly,' she said, 'The police are after you. They knew who they were looking for, believe me. They were flashing a picture of you about. Artist's reconstruction, ha!'

'But I must get in somehow,' he said desperately. The less he had to go on the more anxious he got.

'Can I try phoning my mother from here?'

Ginny looked scornful.

'They'll trace you,' she said. 'Bet if they think it's you they've got the phone tapped already.'

'But I must do something,' he said wearily.

'Look,' said Ginny. 'Don't worry about it now. Come and eat and we'll try and see what we can work out afterwards.'

He tried to walk across the room and found his legs betraying him, folding under him so that Robert had to grab him and lower him carefully onto the chair that the mother had vacated. Ginny was right. He'd have to worry about it later. He suddenly thought of something that had puzzled him.

'Where did you get the mice?'

Ginny giggled. 'They're Neil's pet mice. He's up there getting them all back in their cage now. Maggie's a dreadful liar. All that poison was just aniseed balls.'

Chapter 9

It was an hour later and he felt much stronger. Robert brought him back his oxygen pack mended.

The hands fixing the tubing carefully into the shunt on his chest were square and brown and capable. He had short curly brown hair and vivid blue eyes which he lowered shyly.

'I tried it on myself,' he said, 'just to make sure it was all right. I had to use an old valve but it seems to be working OK.'

'That's brilliant,' Jake said. And then, 'It's very good of you. After all, you don't know me.' He could even have been a murderer, he thought, for all that they knew.

'You're all right,' said Robert reading his thoughts. 'Come and eat.'

His legs functioned rather better this time and with Robert's help he made it down the three flights of the rather dark stairwell without any trouble. There were strange and wonderful smells coming from the kitchen, a large old-fashioned place such as he had only ever seen in history programs, with a large scrubbed table in the centre and all sorts of implements for cutting and peeling and cooking, on side cupboards and walls. Nothing like the little trays of food which he just slid into the wave cooker at home.

Ginny's mother smiled grimly.

'Hungry?'

He realised he was.

'Terribly.'

Her face broke into a surprisingly sweet smile.

The family were all coming in, Maggie, cleaning a sort of dark powdery stuff from her fingers, Ginny and Neil, whom Jake recognised as the one who had helped carry him to the loft hiding place, and finally the father, dressed in an old fashioned zack suit, a dark blue in colour and with the thousands of pockets and the slit sleeves. He nodded at Jake. 'My name's Zed,' he said. 'I understand you're Jake.' His rather stern features cracked into what was almost a smile. 'I hope you'll enjoy your enforced stay with us, Jake.'

They all sat down round the table and he sat on the bench next to Robert while Ginny and Neil brought on steaming pots of food, piles of green cabbage, and root vegetables, even he noted a potato, as well as the soystuff, and a side salad with amazingly lifelike lettuce leaves.

How did they manage to eat like this? They must somehow get it on the black market. Most people only ate genetically engineered food.

He had taken his fork in his hand and cut into the strange textured potato when he realised that nobody else was eating and that Ginny and Neil were sitting with their heads bowed.

'It is our custom,' said Ginny's mother. 'You must not feel obliged to join us.'

The father bowed his head and the rest of the family did likewise.

'To Rakia, thanks.'

'To Rakia, thanks,' chorused the family, raising their heads again.

'Tuck in,' said Ginny.

So they were Rakia's People, he thought. One of the many small Nature sects that had grown up after the Great Plague. It was said that the Nature sects were all mad, if not precisely bad: no makeup, no genetically engineered food, no dancing, no medicine.

'This food looks wonderful,' said Jake.

'Maggie grows it for us.'

Jake nearly choked. He thought glumly of all the probable nasties in food grown without the benefit of the sophisticated tests which market gardeners were required to use by law, poisons which people had believed were safe to put on growing plants years ago and which now were killing them. This food was probably riddled with them. On the other hand nobody in the family looked that ill so he might as well tuck in as instructed. The taste was wonderful as well.

Zed was speaking, his face sombre. 'I have just come from Mineotts, mother. They have bought Lagon home.'

She sighed. 'It's so sad,' she said. 'If only he had listened.'

The faces were dark, depressed.

Ginny's mother must have seen the questioning look on Jake's face for she added, 'Lagon's a young cousin of ours from Mineotts. His father and mother died when he was quite young and he went to live with his aunt. Mineotts is really a Stater area, but many of the friends live there. I know we live in Stater towns but we try to keep separate. Many of our people work.' She looked proudly at Robert. 'Robert has had a job for years. Staters don't seem able to keep them.'

Jake knew that one or two Staters were taken each year by charities and given jobs but the scheme had never had much success.

'Lagon used to keep company with the Staters. We warned him. A day or two ago he went with a gang of them to hold up a lightrail. He was soft on one of their women. He'd have done anything for her.'

Maggie said in her rasping voice, 'Bad associations corrupt good habits. We told him.'

Jake said, 'I know what happened. I was there.'

'They say he must have died quickly. The woman hid his body before the police got there and now they have brought him home.'

'Well, at least Carella will be able to use his allowance for a time that way,' said Ginny's mother practically, and then, looking at Jake, 'Poor Jake, we don't wish to depress you with our troubles. You have troubles enough of your own. Let's talk about other things. Will you have some more salad?'

And unable to resist the fresh clean unadulterated taste Jake had some more.

After the meal Maggie showed him her garden. It was laid out on the roof of the apartment block, bedded down on what must once have been a roof parking area, dating from the time when nearly everyone had a car. Now, of course, private cars were not allowed. The tinted glass overhead was a hodgepodge of different sized pieces, clearly a collection of the broken sections from other long destroyed glasshouses and looking more like a crazily paved stained glass ceiling than anything else. But it was effective. Underneath was a small forest of greenery, rows of leeks and carrots, peas and beans, plants swarming up trellises and under the glass roof, big brightly coloured flowers and vines, several vegetables that Jake had never seen before, and even in one corner a small apple tree.

'Up here,' said Maggie, 'the Staters can't get at it. They just wreck the gardens if they can get at them.'

'What have you used for soil?' he asked. 'Surely it's not possible to purchase soil for a glasshouse this size. You'd need to be a millionaire.'

He remembered the talk by Sandy Stewart the previous week on the Love Canal Syndrome, named after one of the first observed instances of soil contamination in the twentieth century. A thousand poisonous wastes had been dumped in a disused canal near the Niagara Falls in Runa Two and then it had been filled in and built over. The poisons had crept insidiously up and out, into the air, into the houses, killing, maiming and deforming, destroying the plant life, animals and people who lived on it or near it. One large tract in the tropical Enclave of Runa Five had suddenly begun to die, despite all the efforts of Ecopro to save it – where once there had been lush greenery there was now only desert waste – and this had happened not just once but twice on different continents.

'The brothers bring the soil,' said Maggie. 'Every week a small bag. It's exhausted soil from the glasshouses where they work, but at least its poison free. We keep separate from the other Staters and if there's any seasonal work in the glass houses they tend to call on us. The brothers are reliable and we are known to be good at growing things. I make my own compost from our left over food. It's taken us years but now all Rakia's People can eat their own produce. It's better than that engineered rubbish that you all eat.'

Pulling up a radish, she casually brushed off the dirt and said, 'Eat it.'

He did and as the white and red flesh crunched between his teeth and the taste spurted into his mouth he knew that what she said was true.

'Some of the older ones still eat meat when they can,' she said, 'but I don't. The soy stuff's good enough for me and I can actually grow quite a few beans and lentils myself.' She sighed, 'Mark you, I do miss a bit of real bread. You won't ever have tasted that. It was made from a sort of grass called wheat. Soyflour bread just isn't the same.'

Robert appeared next to them, grinning his friendly, lop-sided grin. 'Is Maggie boring you to death with organic compost and the like.'

'You eat the results quite happily,' said the old lady sharply.

'Too right,' said Robert. 'I'm sorry, Maggie, I've come to bear him away. We need to find out what's going on. Let's go and see if we can contact any of your friends, Jake.' And he was dragged away, crunching on a second radish.

Ginny phoned for him, pretending to be a school colleague who needed some information on the French Revolution. Margie thought he was staying with Allie and gave them her number. Allie's mother was very friendly and seemed quite prepared to maintain the fiction that Jake was staying with them for she said that she'd let Jake know that 'Ginny was it?' had called. Allie, she said, was at the ERC. Jake tried her wristcom but she did not respond.

They held a council of war in the kitchen around the big table. Jake had taken them into his confidence and they had started debating what should be done.

Robert had volunteered to go round to Harry's to check what had happened there. If he had returned then Jake would have a free hand to go to the police. Jake still had Harry's key amongst the collection of keys attached to his belt – the people who had robbed him had not bothered with these – and luckily he could remember the code which stood in for the palm recognition procedure.

He was just handing Robert the key when he was suddenly aware of someone moving in the open doorway which led to the central courtyard of the unit. It was a young man of about eighteen or nineteen, swaying on his feet, one side of his face covered in blood.

'Oh Clint, what's happened to you?' said Ginny, horrified, going to fetch him into the room.

'Staters,' he said, 'Staters.'

He had strange blotched skin and his face twitched. There was clearly something wrong with him. Jake knew that it was said that in every Stater home there was an idiot in the back room. It was usually due to lack of oxygen or, conversely, too much. Faulty valves on the oxygen packs were often to blame.

Ginny carefully cleaned his face and he stood obediently like a small child suffering her ministrations.

'There you are. It's actually quite a small cut.'

'Stater,' he said.

'Yes, Clint, aren't they horrible?' She turned to look at Jake. 'They throw stones at him. Just sit down, Clint,' she said gently and then pointing to Jake, 'This is Jake.'

Clint looked at Jake and then turned his back on him, ignoring him, and drew up his legs under his chin and looked at the wall.

'Don't let him worry you. He's not at all dangerous.'

'He was like this when he came back from the Enclave,' said Robert.

'You don't know that,' said Ginny's mother sharply, going past on her way to the back room. 'You don't know that he was at the Enclave at all. Perhaps it was his oxygen valve.' She swept on out.

'And perhaps not,' said Robert shrugging a little. 'Anyway, carry on, Jake. I still don't know why you're so desperate to get into the Enclave.

Jake considered carefully. 'Well, the photograph we found was taken in an Enclave. It said so. And then there's the card. Harry went to the trouble to send it to me and it's something to do with Ecopro. Sandy was terrified to speak to me and he's been killed and it looks as if someone is trying to frame me for it. Harry's missing and his place has been wrecked....

'....And if you wanted to hide someone the Enclave would be a good place to do it since no one is allowed in,' concluded Ginny triumphantly.

He grinned. 'Yes. I don't have enough to go on to convince the police that there's something wrong at Ecopro. But if I can get into their Research Unit I might be able to find out and if I get in while Stick is there he can get into their computer for me. He'll be going with Allie tomorrow, assuming he hasn't found some more lucrative pastime.'

'Rape and Pillage,' said Clint suddenly. He dribbled slightly.

'Yes,' said Ginny soothingly. 'It's all right, Clint.'

'Perhaps if Harry's back at home now we'll have no more problems. I'll be able to go to the police and we'll get the whole matter cleared up. But if he's still missing then I feel I must get into the Enclave.'

Clint began to chant in a cheerful voice:

'Better be a bird not a hen, better be a rabbit
Not a dog. But best of all be a fish.
Better be a mouse, not a mouser, better be a swallow
Not a sheep. But best of all be a fish.

He looked at Jake and smiled innocently. 'Jake,' he said.

'Yes that's right,' said Ginny. 'Jake.'

'Best be a fish.' said Clint. Then he looked frightened and began to whimper. 'Don't want to go into the tunnel,' he said. 'Don't want to play games.'

Ginny's mother came and took him. 'Come on, Clint,' she said gently, 'Time for bed. You mother will be waiting for you.'

He looked at her puzzled for an instant and then smiled radiantly. 'Bedtime. Stories.'

'That's right,'

'Bye, Jake,' he said.

Robert had left to go to Harry's and Ginny was next door reading Clint a story while Jake sat alone in his room. He was beginning to wonder if any of his efforts were worth it. It seemed almost pointless to try further. He was reasonably certain that his father had accepted money as a bribe. The people who had attacked him had got the card and the photograph so there was no evidence of any kind. Allie had the formula, it was true, but that wasn't much help, since it was not for the same product.

The thought of Allie brought her face home to him in a rush, the smooth curve of her cheekbone, the brown eyes alive with intelligence and wit, the tall shapely figure.

He tried again on the wristcom.

He heard her voice, warm and tranquil, saying, 'Hi! Allie here!' and had said 'Hi Allie, it's Jake,' when there was a click at the other end as she turned the phone off. He rang again and again but she didn't answer. He looked at the phone feeling slightly ill and then tore it from his wrist and threw it across the room.

She hadn't even wanted to let him explain. She hadn't given him any chance to defend himself. She had just rung off.

'Oh Allie,' he thought.

'Come on, glum bum,' said Ginny, bursting into the room, 'don't look so doleful. I've just talked to my mother.' Her large dark eyes sparkled with enthusiasm. 'We might just be able to get you into the Enclave. You'll have to go to a meeting though.'

Jake no longer cared.

Chapter 10

They were gathered in the kitchen, the young ones playing a form of draughts, Ginny and Neil watching a game show on an old-fashioned tablet. Ginny was giggling.

A large powerful man opened the door and stepped into the room and a silence fell on the gathering. He was dressed in the kind of suit that was now only seen on archive film, a two piece consisting of a severe black jacket with lapels and buttons and trousers of the same material, a white shirt and black tie, also now totally outmoded, and black shoes. He had a small black plastic bag in his hand.

Everybody looked down and appeared uncomfortable. Only Ginny's mother seemed unperturbed, finishing washing the lettuce and putting it on a plate, before wiping her hands and putting them together in a prayer like position over her stomach.

'Greetings, Threskay. You are well?

'Greetings, Sister, I am well.' He nodded at the assembled company and the two smaller children slipped from the room. Ginny and Neil also made the small prayer like movement in greeting and then stood with eyes cast down, waiting. The great plain face was stern and unyielding as he inspected Jake calmly.

'This is the young visitor?'

Ginny's mother nodded and said, 'His name is Jake. It seems that injustice has been done.'

'Ah!' Although he was plainly a powerful man his complexion was grey and he looked almost suffering. 'The police came.'

'They came, Threskay. They found nothing. They are gone. Will you eat with us tonight?'

He smiled and for a moment he looked almost human.

'Thank you but no. I have more calls to make.' He looked at Jake again and said, 'So you are visiting us, Jake? How does life look to one who, I suspect, enjoys rather better circumstances at home?'

'Ginny and her family have been very helpful and kind,' said Jake.

This seemed to please him for he smiled again. 'Do you follow the path?'

How do you answer that, thought Jake. 'I have not been instructed, Sir. I do not know the path.'

The great plain face was sad. 'Many do not know the path. Hence the world we see. I should be pleased to see you at the meeting.' He turned to Ginny's mother. 'I look forward to seeing you tonight, Sister.' He paused and seemed to search for a way of putting his next remark tactfully but found none. It came out like stone. 'He is not one of us, Sister. If it should bring ostracism on the brethren then it would be wise for him to leave. Some have complained. The police are not scrupulous in their attacks.'

'I shall bear it in mind, Threskay. And we shall come to the meeting.'

The suffering eyes once again tried to smile. 'I have brought some soil for Maggie. Give her my greetings.'

'It will be my pleasure,' said Ginny's mother respectfully, as he put the small bag down on a chair beside the door, and she closed the door quietly behind him. Everybody breathed a sigh of relief when he had gone and even Ginny's mother seemed more relaxed. 'They do a great deal of good, you know,' she said, rather defensively, 'This would be a terrible area if it weren't for their influence. And they help us a lot with the food and gardens.' She thought about it. 'Maggie would have been a Threskay if she had been a man.'

It was unusual, Jake thought, to find the men wielding such power, although he knew that this had been the case in the early history of the human race. It was unjust, really, the way all the best jobs now usually went to women. Women were society's leaders. The power shift had been subtle. It had occurred when people had first been able to choose whether to have a boy or a girl. At first the balance had been heavily in favour of boys, especially in the lower number Runas and even, surprisingly in Runa One. But as these choices had worked their way through to the new generation it was left with insufficient womenfolk and suddenly women were more desirable. Coupled with their undoubted efficiency with this desirableness came power.

Now they were in the ascendancy. The shift had been irrevocable. Allie would be one of the world's leaders. But Allie, he thought, with her wit and charm and beauty would have been a leader anyway.

And now Allie didn't want to speak to him any more. Not since the police wanted to interview him to 'eliminate him from their enquiries.'

The door banged back again and Robert came swinging through. 'I've been to your father's place.' He fished in his pocket. 'There's the key. It looks as if someones's been in already and tidied it up. No sign of any break in, papers in a neat pile on the desk, cupboards back in place and so on. I collected your package.' He handed it over. 'It was where you said it would be. I got chatting to the chap in the next unit – a right old busybody – and asked if your father had been back but he said he was pretty sure not, but that some strange people had been round twice. He wanted to know what I'd been doing there and so I said I was the plumber and that the chap in the unit below had reported a leak. I asked him if he was from the condo committee and if so what had happened to my money and that seemed to scare him off all right.'

He grinned. 'And I also dropped the note in for your hacker friend. Some bird there with pink hair said he was down at the central library with your friend Allie.'

Once again he felt the sharp rush of jealousy and despair. He should have been there with Allie. And she was no longer his friend. She didn't want to speak to him. What, he wondered, was she doing keeping company with Stick. If only she had let him explain.

As if a reflection of his thoughts he heard his wristcom ring and threw himself across the room to answer it.

'Yes, he said, yes.'

The voice was still cynical and worldly wise but Stick was quick and concise. 'I got your message. We've made one or two discoveries. Allie won't phone you because she thinks her phone is being voice traced, and after this call neither will I. If there's any possible way you can join us at the Enclave that would help but don't run any risks. We'll let you know afterwards what happens. Over and out.'

His heart lifted and sang. They were still with him. They would go to the Enclave. She hadn't answered because of the voice trace.

But it meant he couldn't contact her. He could see her now, the soft blond hair swinging, the large brown eyes concerned and worried. She would go to the Enclave tomorrow with Stick. He had to get there. Ginny had said that the elders, these Threskay, or whatever they were called, might be able to get him in and although he couldn't really see how it was almost his only option. The meeting was at eight o'clock. The time would pass slowly.

They set off at half past seven. He had only known Ginny in her workaday clothes and was amazed at how different she looked in the clean jump suit, with the puffy sleeved blouse tucked into the tiny waist, hair brushed and shining but still floating around her face in an unruly cloud.

They walked as a group, the men forming a front and rear guard; and Jake noticed that Robert surreptitiously carried a small stun gun.

After about a half and hour of winding between the high walls of Stater units, interspersed with derelict houses and patches of waste ground, they eventually came to a small hill. About halfway up there was a smallish building set back from the road on the rim of the hillside. He gradually realised as they went down some steps to the front door that most of the building must be below ground level. The windows at the front were covered with heavy metal bars, and this, coupled with the building's height, gave the place a squat, grim, forbidding aspect.

Ginny's mother saw him looking at them and said, 'Many people do not know the Path. Staters have broken in several times and destroyed the meeting place.'

The doorposts were in the form of two massive trees trunks, the door between them also covered with wire mesh. They knocked and after a while someone within opened it to the width of one person. He nodded at them welcomingly as they passed him one at a time, stopping short when he got to Jake.

He looked at him carefully. 'Are you a brother?' he asked.

Ginny, who was in front of Jake, turned and said, 'No, Jimmy, he's a friend. Let him in. He's with us.'

An unexpectedly large shoulder prevented Jake from moving forward. 'I think I must check with the Threskay. If you wouldn't mind waiting here, friend.'

Jake was about to say that it hadn't been his idea to come and if they didn't want him they had only to say so but at that moment a small fussy man, also dressed in the same old fashioned suit and black tie as the man who had come to the house, appeared.

'A new friend.' said the doorkeeper.

The man had a round face with a receding hairline from which a lot of brown curls were swept back, a small mouth with slightly protruding teeth, and eyes which instead of being set deep in their sockets appeared to be right at the surface of face. There was a small mole just below his chin and his smile was affectionate and insincere.

'That is wonderful to hear. But, of course, we must know who sponsors you. There are those who really wish to follow the path but ... We have many enemies...'

The large elder whom he had met first appeared and nodded at Jake unsmilingly.

'Welcome, friend. I am glad that you could come.'

'Oh, if you know Threskay Van Rijk that's all right then.' The round faced elder looked a little irritated. 'Ginny will look after you I'm sure.'

They were in a small entrance hall and someone took his parka and he noticed Robert handing over his stun gun. They stepped down more steps and came through the final door onto a sort of balcony. The squat exterior had not prepared him for the sense of height and lightness. It was like stepping into a clearing in a forest, surrounded on all sides by what appeared to be the trunks of trees with light playing through the leaves from above.

It was, he realised, a hall similar to an old fashioned cinema with the almost all encircling screen around them onto which images of trees and greenery were being projected. It was not at all like a church. There was no altar, no cross, no images, only everywhere the marvellous and glowing trees. It was like walking into a forest as they were escorted to their places.

Threskay van Rijk stood in front of a display of moving leaves and blue sky projected onto the back wall, the lights dimmed until they were all bathed in glowing green and yellow light, and then he raised his arms and they began to sing.

Looking round Jake saw that many were handicapped, some blind, some lame, some clearly brain damaged by malfunctioning oxygen equipment, and many with the leprous skin blotches caused by the contaminated food and water, and skin cancers. But the voices rose pure and clear, a thin, eerie song, almost a chant, to the great god of the trees.

Glory be for all living things

Praise be for all green things
Praise be for growth, for food, for life

The women and children took up the refrain and the thin clear sound echoed round and round the hall, the faces of the singers ecstatic.

The silence which followed was absolute and then van Rijk began to speak.

'It is said, brothers and sisters, that man was created from Rakia's tears and that we are but reflections in the mirror of the Great Being. We know that if we drop something into that pool we distort the image. That something, brothers, is sin.'

Jake scarcely listened, hearing only the odd sentence here and there. How could Ginny have thought that these poor souls could get him into the Enclave? They were the underclass, the rejected of humanity. What could they do?

The sermon seemed to go on for hours and Jake began to sweat. Time was running out on him. They sang again and then there was a further minute's contemplation.

As the meeting broke up Ginny's mother called him to the back of the hall, to a small door set behind a mural of the two great tree trunks, and as he went through she whispered to him, 'Good luck.'

Inside was a small committee room with five men gathered round a table. The large elder who had visited the house, Threskay van Rijk, said, 'Greetings friend.' and the others murmured greetings also.

'Greetings, friends,' he said as Ginny had prompted him. He was now cold with nerves.

The elder at the head of the table was a small man with soft brown hair and an old fashioned moustache.

'I am Threskay van Holt. Would you like to tell us your name, friend?'

'Jake. Jake Delagard.'

'And how do you come to be in the Downtown Kington Estate?'

'I was following a man from Ecopro to ...', he thought rapidly. He did not want to tell them his real reason for needing to get into the Enclave... 'to ask about the Enclave. He worked there.'

There was a faintly ominous pause. 'So we understand. This man died, friend.'

'I know nothing about his death,' he said rapidly. 'I was attacked and left unconscious. Ginny and Robert found me. They'll vouch for the fact that the man was all right when they left.'

He looked for the great plain face of the first Threskay. He, at least believed him.

'You must believe me,' he said. 'I had nothing to do with it.'

The round faced elder who had greeted him at the door spoke sympathetically. 'Of course we believe you. However there does seem to be some ...' he paused, 'some misunderstanding with the police, does there not? It would surely be much better for you to go to them yourself and explain things. If, as you say, you have done no wrong then you have nothing to fear.'

'I can't do that at the moment,' he said despairingly, 'I can't tell you why.'

The round faced elder turned to the others. 'I'm sorry, brothers. I feel that our friend, for he is not a brother, is endangering our congregation. Twice we have had the police into the estate. It is unheard of. We are known to the civil authorities for our respect for the law. I will not be party to breaking it.'

The elder with the moustache looked down a moment.

Van Rijk said, 'Neither is it our duty to enforce the law, brother, if there appears some injustice has been done.'

The chairman said, 'True. Such matters should be left to Rakia. It will be resolved in His good time. And...' he looked warningly at the round faced elder, 'neither should any individual Threskay feel that he should take things upon himself to order matters. We will decide as a body.' He turned his gaze to Jake. 'We understand you have a request of the Threskay.'

With his nerves it came out badly. '... I need to get into the Green Enclave. I understand you can help me.'

'You must give us the reason, friend.'

'I can't tell you,' he said, 'the reason is not mine to give but...' he sought desperately for the right words to sway them, 'I do not go to harm. And ... and I will go to the police immediately afterwards, I give you my word.'

'He is not holy,' one said.

'Please. It would be an act of great kindness,' he said.

The elder who had first refused him entrance spoke, the eyes wide in an odd mix of piety and cunning.

'We all know that entry to the Sacred Wood is a holy trust. It should not be endangered for one we do not know. He might be a spy.'

The second Threskay was dismissive. 'This is no spy, brother. All men are entitled to see the Holy Creation. This is not ours to deny. Only if there is a question of safety.'

'The police have come twice. What do they know that we do not? It will endanger the Holy Trust.'

The elder with the moustache pursed his lips and said 'True. We must think this matter through. Go home, young friend, and await our decision.'

'I have only a short time,' he said desperately.

The elder spoke with firm finality, 'Go home now. We will let you know tonight.'

Back at the house he gathered his few things together. He did not trust the round faced elder. He was certain that he would betray him somehow to the police if he could. He must try and get to Allie.

Ginny said, 'Can't you just wait for the elders. I'm sure they'll do it.'

'I can't,' he said desperately. 'Who knows what's happened to my dad. Tell your family thanks for everything. I've left you a package in the bedroom. Perhaps you could give it to Threskay van Rijk for safe keeping. I'll let you know what happens.'

'I'll come with you,' she said. 'Wait.'

He was on the first floor landing when he heard the distant wail of the sirens, the patrol arriving. He had been right: the Threskay had betrayed him. The door at the foot of the stairs opened and four dark figures stood in front of him, their faces in shadow.

'It has been decided,' said the tall powerful figure at the front. 'Come!'

And he was hustled away into the darkness.

Chapter 11

As they reached the back door Robert's voice said gruffly, 'Ye must be blindfolded now. I'm sorry,' and a large soft black cloth was placed over his eyes and tied firmly behind his head.

He stumbled as he was going out of the door but strong hands held him and he was helped outside, feeling the cool evening air on his face. The sirens seemed to be getting louder. He was lifted hastily and laid on his side, squashed firmly against some sacking and a metal wall, heard murmured instructions to keep still, and then was covered with more sacking. He could feel small hard knobbly things pressing into him and something which might have been a trainer was pushed uncomfortably against his face.

'Don't move,' hissed a voice and he was crushed further and further back against the metal wall, cold through the sacking, more people's feet jabbing him in the stomach and sides, the one against his face pressing uncomfortably close to his eye. The metallic whine of an electric motor echoed in his head, something slammed shut and they lurched into movement.

He must be, he thought, in an old-fashioned van or truck, underneath a side bench on which people were sitting. The motor gained in power and they began to move, bumpily, curving round a corner, out of the courtyard, he thought, onto the road. The courtyard must have been flagged in some way and as the vehicle bumped and rocked over the uneven surface he was banged and bruised by the feet, crushed as he was between the wall and the floor of the vehicle. Nobody talked and despite his discomfort he could feel the nervousness. The sirens were now painfully loud.

It was slightly less uncomfortable on the road but only just.

A voice said, 'They are bound to see us.'

And a reply, 'I intend that they should.'

The vehicle rolled to a stop, somebody climbed from the front, and the door slammed.

The first voice said, 'Rakia's Wood, he's flagging them down,' and another said, calmly, confidently, 'Threskay van Rijk knows what he's doing.'

There was a screech of tyres and more doors slamming, and then a voice, loud and irritable, saying, 'Get off the road! Get off the road, man. Are you a total fool? You might have been killed.'

Jake, straining, could only just catch the quiet reply. 'Good evening, brother. I just need your advice.'

A harsh obscenity. 'Don't you brother me. I don't like being deliberately delayed. There's murder been done in this area and we don't need idiots like you holding us up.'

The Threskay said mildly, 'I'm sorry, friend. We are on our way to an assembly of the brethren, as you can see, and when I saw you all I wondered if it was safe to continue. Are there troubles in the area? We are headed towards Mineotts Estate.'

'Mineotts?' thought Jake, 'that's the opposite direction to the Enclave.' He thought for a moment that his hearing was distorted because he could hear a thin humming, rising in volume and making it difficult to catch the conversation outside.

'No troubles that way,' the voice was surly. 'If you come from the Fairfield Estate I must inspect your vehicle.'

The humming was swelling in volume and one or two voices began to quietly add the refrain. It was one of the hymns which he had heard at the meeting hall. Two male voices took the main tune and he could hear Ginny's mother joining the descant.

The doors at the rear slammed opened and the voices fell silent. 'As you can see, friend....'

'Officer Gunway, if you don't mind.'

'..... As you can see, we have the legal minimum of passengers and we take a few fruits and vegetables to our less fortunate brethren. Perhaps you would like some for your fellow officers.' Jake could feel someone moving the bags near his feet. Some of the sacking on his legs began to slide. Don't move them any more, he prayed. He felt a sudden urge to sneeze.

'What have you got? Oh, just onions. Keep the polluted muck. It should suit Mineotts. Come on Hank, let's be going.'

The sound of the boots faded but he heard the voice quite clearly, 'A real bunch of nutters, that lot. They talk to the trees. Thank God I only do this district once in a blue moon.' The door to the police vehicle slammed, someone closed the back door to their vehicle, the motor whined and they moved off. The humming started again and soon they were in full song, relief and joy echoing even through the sacking to Jake.

He sneezed violently, someone laughed, and the hymn continued.

It must have been half an hour later that the van slid to a halt. Everybody, as far as Jake could tell, climbed out and he was dragged unceremoniously from his hidey-hole. He had lost all feeling in the leg and arm on which he had been lying and when they stood him down on the ground he sagged and almost fell. Someone grabbed his arm, saying 'Steady on,' and as he slowly straightened up he caught a whiff of the perfume Ginny had been wearing that afternoon. She was leaning next to him and whispering in his ear, 'So far, so good,' and he only knew that he felt enormously relieved that she was with them.

Ginny, he felt, was on his side.

'I'm sorry about the blindfold,' Robert said again. 'You'll be able to get it off soon. Ye see if we're taken ye must not be able to tell them anything.'

'I don't mind,' he said. 'I'm all right.'

Ginny put her hand in his. 'This way,' she said. 'You go up two steps.'

It was difficult and at first his steps were faltering but then the press of bodies round him carried him along up the steps, into what he judged to be a passageway and then out into a large, cool open area.

'Now two steps down,' said Ginny and then there's a little ledge.' She put an arm round his waist and took him with her.

Now people were crowding round them, they were pushed close together, the smell of bodies in a confined space overwhelming. He put his arm round Ginny pulled her closer to him and smelled the fresh clean smell of her hair.

A voice said, 'That's enough for the first load,' there was a creak and grind of metal grating and something snapping into place, the sound of more machinery and then, suddenly, without warning, they were dropping like a stone and his stomach was empty and compressed, gone in that one sickening, tearing plunge. There was a shriek of pulleys and winches and a rush of cold air and then after what seems like hours of free fall they jolted to a crunching halt.

And then, after more creaking noises, people began to move away from him. He realised that he was clamped to Ginny, still hugging her desperately, and as he slowly separated himself he heard her small giggle. 'We must come here more often.'

Then her hand was taken from his he was pushed forward and Robert was saying, 'You can have the blindfold off now. You'll have to follow on your own; most of the way there's only space for one at a time.'

At first he thought that the blindfold had damaged his eyesight in some way because the darkness before him was just as profound as when he had been wearing it, but then in front of him he caught the flicker of a light and putting out a hand felt to the left of him a wall, cold and damp, carved from rock. To the right, nothing. He was in some sort of passageway.

Another light flickered ahead of him and then another, like small glow-worms in the dark, and he heard Ginny call, 'Are you all right? Come on, it's quite safe. Keep close to the wall or the rails will trip you.'

He put his hand up to a stone wall, feeling again the cold slime, and stepped forward using the lights ahead as his guide. His eyes were gradually adjusting to the darkness, seeing the cavernous passageway ahead of him, the dull gleam of the metal tracks running its length and the carved rock of the walls.

He must be in an old mine, one of those which dated from all those years ago when there was still coal. He stumbled again and Robert thrust a torch into his hand. 'Here,' he said roughly, 'use this.'

Jake looked around uneasily, wondering how safe these mine workings could possibly be after all these years, then saw, in the flickering light of the torch, the new pit props and the piles of rubble which had been swept aside at intervals along the passage. In fact, a considerable amount of work must have gone into restoring the tunnel.

He realised as he made his unsteady way forward that other tunnels branched from this main one, sloping down and away from them, and finally they too branched off into a smaller and less easily negotiated tunnel, where he was obliged to walk with head and back bent. It went on for what seemed like hours, cold and uncomfortable, deeper and deeper into the mine, past more and more smaller tunnels leading off and seemingly endless. How did anyone ever find their way back?

He tripped and had stumbled on for some minutes, looking down at his feet to make sure that he did not trip again, suddenly realising, on looking up, that he could not see the lights ahead. He glanced over his shoulder and saw no lights behind either, and taken with terror began to run, stumbling, head bent, trying to catch up. He would never find his way back. He fell and grazed his hand and ran again, with more and more difficulty as the roof of the tunnel came lower and lower, breathing raggedly, bent nearly double.

And then he heard Robert's voice behind him, 'Steady on, lad. They'll wait for us if need be,' and saw, at the same time, the lights glowing ahead.

They came finally to a smaller tunnel yet, where they merely crawled, but now they were crawling upwards towards a small hole and the gleam of lights.

The hole opened out into a small room carved from the rock, the rim of the hole about three feet from the floor. Someone helped him down.

'Are we all here?' said van Rijk.

Now that all the torches were gathered in one place he could see the faces, eager, happy, expectant. Even the Threskay looked relaxed and almost cheerful.

'Aye,' said Robert. 'I was last.'

'Remember, brothers, we have this one night. Let us use it to the full. We meet again outside an hour before dawn. We cannot be responsible for anyone arriving late.'

He turned to Jake. 'I'm sorry that you must go blindfolded again. Only the faithful know the path.'

'I understand,' said Jake as Robert fastened the band around his eyes.

Once again he was half pushed, half carried forward and then knew that they were out in the open, that the all enclosing stone walls had gone.

'Is everybody out?'

'Make sure it is well covered.'

'Well done.'

He felt a small cold hand slipped into his and smelled again Ginny's perfume. 'They're just covering up the entrance,' she whispered.

Now they were slipping and sliding down an embankment, scree rolling under their feet, Ginny holding him on one side, Robert on the other.

He tried to calculate where they might be. Miles from the Ecopro research station, that was for sure. The old mine was probably one of several near Crater Edge; this one must run into the hill and then out the other side into the Enclave.

Now the ground was levelling out and something soft and spongy was underfoot, something rather like a carpet. They had gone a considerable distance when they stopped again, the blindfold was undone and he was released.

Ginny was tugging at his hand.

'Come and stand here,' she said.

Chapter 12

The first thing he noticed was the coolness and then the movement, the trembling of the leaves above him. Elegant arches of trunks and branches soared over him in the moonlight, mighty trees, fifty, sixty, eighty feet high, the dark green leaves twisting and moving in the air. Under his feet was soft green grass.

This was not the brown wizened vegetation from outside the Enclave. This was alive.

He looked at Ginny, laughed delightedly and looked up again. Tomorrow, he thought, he would have a crick in his neck but he didn't care. It was a full moon and the light played through the lattice work of leaves above him in incredible beauty.

He had never been anywhere like it before, surrounded by a thousand living, breathing trees. Even the giant glasshouses had never had greenery like this. The very air smelled different, cool and moist and clean. A breeze ran through the branches and the leaves rustled. He dragged Ginny across to the tree nearest to him and felt the rough bark beneath his hand.

All the trees in the condo villages were fenced off, not to be touched, and anyway they were nothing like these, but poor things struggling to survive beneath the tinted glass of the condo quadrangles. He breathed deeply, drawing the cool, clean air into his lungs.

They were being called forward to stand in a circle round Van Rijk. The torches had been extinguished and the only light was the silver river from the full moon. Everyone was silent.

'How did they find it?' he whispered to Ginny.

'It was by accident really', she said. 'They were just looking for the black fuel. Many of the brothers don't have heating in their houses in the same way as in the condo villages and in the winter it's really too cold to go without fire. Someone discovered that there were one of two knobs of the black fuel on the ground near the entrance to a cave on Crater Edge but as time went on they had to go further and further in to find anything. And then, one day they found the central mineshaft with the lift.

Some of our men managed to get it going again. The black fuel is dirty, of course, so we only use it sparingly but then, one day they found the exit. It was a gift from Rakia.

'Do you believe in this Rakia?'

Ginny smiled. 'It would be silly not to believe at all, wouldn't it? See how much better everything is if you do as the Threskay say. My second name is Jasidh, that means loyalty.'

Yes, he thought, Ginny would be loyal.

The crowd pressed in a tighter circle around the Threskay and Ginny kept tight hold of his hand and drew him into the group. They were chanting the song thing again, the voices thin and clear and cold, rising eerily into the dark boughs above them. He had visited a cathedral once, to attend a memorial service for a dead colleague of his mother's. The great vaulted branches reminded him of the cathedral and they had sung a song like this at the service, of sadness, of loss, of the destruction of all that was good.

He shivered.

Now they chanted the responses that he had heard at the hall.

'Glory for all living things,
Praise for all green things Praise be to Rakia.'

He listened and was moved.

'Aren't you afraid someone will hear you?' he asked Ginny.

'No,' said Ginny. 'Not now. We did at first. We just came and stood and then went back again. But as time went on we realised no one could hear us. The only danger is from the research centre and they never come into the Holy Wood at night now.

They used to once. Several of the brothers used to work at the Centre before the new Director came and they told us when the night patrols were due. But they haven't had them for years; since the outer fences have proved so effective there wasn't much need for them to worry about the wood at night.

'And anyway,' she said proudly, 'they have no cause to fear our people. We don't need to touch the trees to worship. It is enough that they are there.'

The singing was continuing. Everyone was absorbed, rapt.

'Ginny,' he whispered, 'I must go.'

She was, he realised, still holding his hand and she led him out into a small clearing away from the gathering. The thin ghostly music pursued them through the trees.

She tugged at this hand so that he was in the middle of the clearing and with her free hand pointed upward. 'Do you know which one is the North Star. Can you see it? '

Jake nodded. The air of the Enclave seemed to heighten the perfume from her hair and skin and the moon made her eyes seem larger and brighter than ever.

'The enclave is aligned east to west to catch the sun. If you keep the North Star on your right hand you will come to the research centre. You can't miss it. Just before you get there there is a huge clearing, with a couple of lines of trees on the far side. I think it's a fire break, and on this side of the clearing there are two sets of trip wires. They're set quite high so that they miss most of the animals. Once you're past those and the clearing we believe you're in the experimental area, although we don't know.

Ginny shivered. 'I wish you weren't going.'

'I'll be all right.' He wished he felt as confident as he sounded.

'Remember you've sworn not to reveal how you got in.'

'I honestly don't have the vaguest idea, so that won't be difficult,' he said. 'I must go.'

'Let me come with you,' she said suddenly.

'No, you mustn't,' he said with determination. 'I'd like you with me. Ginny, but it's far too dangerous. And it's not your war. Thank you anyway.'

He released her hand and something light and soft brushed against his cheek; and then she was scampering away into the darkness and he was left alone.

'No, wait,' he wanted to say, but she had gone.

He waited for a few moments, then checked his position with the North Star, turned his face resolutely to the east and set off. It was, he adjudged, about ten miles to the Research Centre. He had to get there before dawn when, presumably, the staff would begin to arrive and there would be more patrols than at night. He would have to run.

The grass was soft beneath his feet and he made practically no sound as he padded along between the trees. They were well spaced and at first his progress was easy. Above him the branches danced and played and the breeze was refreshingly cool as he kept up the pace, glancing occasionally upward to check his position.

As time went on the breeze became stronger, turning to wind which whipped the tree tops to frenzy and swept huge clouds across the moon, and then large cold drops splashed down. He ignored the rain and continued his run, keeping to an easy stride. The wind came in little gusts, lashing the rain against his face, soaking his face and hair and clothes. He realised that he had almost never been caught out in rain before and put his face up to the wind and felt the cool drops on his face.

He must have been running for nearly an hour. Something was bothering him slightly and he realised that it was the absolute silence, that he could not hear the puff and click of his oxygen pack. In fact, now he came to think about it, he could not remember having heard it since he came into the Enclave. He swung his pack off and checked the gas level but it was still over a third full and the test system showed that it was functioning perfectly. This is what life must have been like before the Blind Ages, when people could breathe the air of the planet without suffocating. He could not believe how fresh the air smelled.

The wind had died again and the moon provided a skylit alley between the trees as he jogged steadily on.

Suddenly, out of the corner of his eye, he saw something move and slowed and swerved close to a tree and stopped. He saw the movement again and just beyond him in a large clearing something white flicked and was gone.

They were rabbits, perhaps five or six of them, small brown rabbits, nibbling contentedly at the grass, black in the moonlight, moving their noses, sitting, ears pricked, scudding away as his arm brushed a branch and rained a small shower of glistening moonlit drops to the ground below.

It was rare to see animals these days. Some large domestic beasts were kept by farmers in special stalls, one or two carefully selected and cloned animals that never saw the light of day. There was little enough food for humans, let alone for animals. He had never seen animals wandering in the open air before. It seemed strange.

There was another movement on the far side of the clearing and a large ruffed dog head lifted above the long grass. It was a fox. Jake watched entranced. It made no attempt to move as the rabbits jumped and nibbled and sniffed the air of the clearing. Jake reckoned he still had about a quarter of an hour before he got near to the Research Centre so he had a little time in hand. No one would arrive before dawn, surely, and it was so peaceful here.

A small breeze ruffled the surface of the grass and one of the rabbits, lifted its head, sniffed the air, and ran. The fox was bounding after it, the plumed tail streaming behind, disappearing towards the trees on the far side of the clearing.

There was a small sound. The fox lifted in the air, spun, turned slowly and then dropped and lay. The white of the rabbit's tail disappeared into the shrubbery beyond the edge of the clearing.

At first Jake, could not understand it. Then, in horror, realised that he had miscalculated. He was at the Centre. These were the first alarm systems. He heard the sound of voices and two women strolled out from between the trees, guns over their arms.

'Ah tis just a fox,' said one. 'I thought it must be by the size of the charge. We'd better take a quick look round.' Jake froze.

He was still there, rigid against the tree, a quarter of an hour later. The women had inspected the area around the fox carefully, coming right across the clearing to near where he stood, shining their torches between the trees, but they had not seen him.

'Well, he won't chase any more rabbits, I guess,' said one, moving the fox slightly with her boot.

'Save 'em for you, won't it.'

'Ah, it's good sport. Helps to keep your eye in. Better than those useless targets down at the range.' The woman looked around the clearing and said, 'There's usually a few about here.'

As if to prove her words a small rabbit hopped casually into the circle of light beneath the trees and began to nibble cautiously at the grass.

'You must admit, they're cute,' said the second guard.

'Very,' said the first, bringing up her gun and firing low from the hip. The rabbit's head disintegrated.

'Good shot. Do you know if Kurosaka does her rounds early today? I'm hoping to get away at twelve because I've got Sammy coming for lunch.' The voice became admonishing, 'And you know they don't like us using those things unless we have to.'

Their voices faded into the silvery mist between the trees.

Only then did he dare to move, slowly and cautiously, back away from the trip wires and the invisible barrier, away from the dead rabbit and the smell of blood, back into the safety of the Enclave.

Clearly he needed to plan his way forward. It was amazing that the Station itself was so well guarded. That the trees themselves should need protection he understood. Allow anybody in to picnic and set fires and the work of fifty years could be undone in an hour. But why should the station itself need to be so shielded?

The trip wires were easy to find, the silver metal shining in the moonlight where they had been exposed by the small animals which had come up against them. But the invisible barrier was much more dangerous, probably some sort of electric charge screen, activated by a photo cell, a laser beam of some kind. Somehow he was going to have to get past it if he hoped to get into the central buildings.

The rabbit he thought had got under the screen but the fox had been too big. A refrain rang in his head like music. Was it a clue, he thought?

Better be a bird not a hen, better be a rabbit not a dog. A dog was much like a fox.

The cracked voice of the idiot at Ginny's came back to him. Better be a bird, Clint had sung.

Why a bird? So that you could fly over the top of the screen, of course. Hens didn't fly much. Unfortunately neither could he. But was it possible that there were some trees which overhung the screen. Probably they would cut them off but it was worth checking.

He followed the clearing round for as long as he dared but eventually began to despair. The clearing must encircle the Centre completely and there were no trees on this side of the screen. Or where he imagined the screen must be since presumably it ran through the clearing where the laser eye could travel freely.

He came to a stream and began to wade across it. Light was beginning to creep into the sky, a thin sliver of pale yellow shading the distant horizon. Time was running out. Dawn was breaking. He heard the voice again in his head.

Be a bird, he thought, but not a hen, be a rabbit but not a fox, but best of all be a fish.

The water! Clint had found the way in.

Then Jake shivered. Look at what had happened to Clint.

Chapter 13

Back in the safety of the trees he quickly removed his clothes, making them into a neat bundle. Creeping as close as he dared to the dead fox, to where he imagined the screen might be, he hurled the bundle up as high as he could, up and over the screen and then raced back for the cover of the trees. He waited another ten minutes. No guards, no rabbit killers appeared. His clothes must be safe on the other side.

The sky was much lighter and now tinged with red and grey as he headed towards the stream looking down to where he imagined the screen must be. He would need to get right to the big willow curving in over the water on the far side to be sure of missing it. Probably if he kept his head below the level of the stream banks he would be OK since the laser eyes would have to travel in straight lines across the top. Unless there were any set actually in the banks of the stream.

The water was quite shallow but icy cold and took his breath away as he lay down in the deepest part, the water washing around him. It was not deep enough to swim and so he pulled himself along by the reeds at the sides, virtually crawling along the bottom of the stream bed. As he came near to the spot where the screen must be he kept his face and body below the surface of the water and pulled himself forward, feeling the clear cold water wash over him, his body scraping the stones at the base of the bed. He did not know how long he had been going without air. He did not dare look up. And then something touched the back of his head and brushed along his back and in a start of terror he reared up out of the water, realising with relief that he had got to the willow.

A little further on he crawled out onto the grass. The trees were thicker on this side of the screen and there was more undergrowth so that it took him some time to find his clothes and put them on again, fastening his oxygen pack back into the shunt, his hands unwilling to do what he wanted them to, his teeth chattering with the cold. Eventually he was ready to go, wondering which direction he should take and how many more shields he would come to before he was safe. He put his jacket on a long branch and held it stretched before him in the hopes that it would hit any screen before he did and then that the charge would not hurt him at a distance.

The grass grew long on this side and there were fewer trees. He came across a track worn into the grass and set off along it, still heading east, into the rising sun. If people used the track, he thought, then presumably at least along its length there were no screens.

He noticed the first dead tree within minutes, and then another and then another. At first it was just one here and there amongst the good wood but then there were more and more of them, some completely blighted, with blackened branches from which bark hung in thin wispy strips, some clearly dying with browned leaves and curling twisted tips at the branch ends. It was like a graveyard.

But, he thought, it wasn't possible. This was still a magnetically shielded area. What had happened to these trees. He was half conscious that the sun was in the sky, burning down, and that he had neither visor nor cream to protect himself, that the wonderful life giving greenery was gone.

What had happened. The area stretched for about a mile, and as he progressed further and further down the track his sense of desolation grew. It looked as if a forest fire had passed through some years before leaving only these terrible blackened stumps around which the new grass grew.. But it was not a fire. Each tree, Jake found as he looked at the ones closest to the track, was covered with a thin film of fungus-like material, tiny bubbles of white and yellow, packed into every crevice of the bark. The trees were diseased.

And then, suddenly, he remembered the other areas where Enclaves had failed. In Runa Five and Runa Eight. And he felt the beginnings of despair. Even with all the modern equipment, the protective shields, the research units, they still could not keep the forest alive.

It meant they were all doomed. He felt cold despite the heat of the sun.

The track branched and he could see, ahead of him, a series of outhouse type buildings, and, beyond them, the taller units of the labs and the control area. He must not be spotted here. He thought again of what had happened to Clint and felt the familiar sickness in the pit of his stomach. Veering from the track, he plunged into the long grass and crawled to the edge of the path leading to the most distant and smallest of the outbuildings. Perhaps this was where the guards came from.

But no. The buildings looked quite deserted as he approached them, one with a door hanging open, the path to it overgrown. He sidled to the edge of the building and looked round. Nothing moved, no sound, only the hum of insects in the grass. Beyond the hut was what looked like an old allotment garden, similar to Maggie's but now completely neglected and run to seed.

Made bold by the silence and the unkempt air of the place Jake slipped inside and looked around. It appeared to have been a base for the scientists doing field work, for there were clip boards and a notice board with a faded list of names; and hanging behind the door was an old white coat. There was also a small, hand embroidered sampler on the wall saying:

To Rakia, Praise

One of the brothers worked here once, thought Jake. Undoubtedly it was his allotment and perhaps he was one of those who had been dismissed, inexplicably, by the new Director so that the little garden had been given over to the weeds.

Ten minutes later, clad in the coat and carrying one of the clipboards, with his head well down, Jake headed for the main buildings. Two women passed him, the first giving him a curious look, the second ignoring him completely, neither, he thought, as his heart lifted, raising the alarm.

He passed what was obviously a new plantation with rows of small trees, and came at last to the main area. The central set of buildings was in the shape of a giant pentagon with the various buildings along each side of the five sides, some only single storey but some four or five floors high, clearly housing labs and office departments. Between each of the buildings were covered walkways, with rambling plants and more greenery.

He needed somewhere to hide until Stick and Allie arrived. Heading down one of the covered walkways, he followed a little sign saying Shield Machinery and discovered a single storey building with great double doors at the front and a small door in the side. It had, however, a palm print procedure box at the side so he knew it was no use trying there. He carried on round the path on the inside of the pentagon. More and more people were using the pathways and he noticed that they all had a small badge with some sort of insignia, undoubtedly a security clearance tag. Stick and Allie were coming today here today. They'd be issued one.

His chest began to feel naked and bare. He noticed a second person look at him curiously and knew that he would have to hide quickly. This disguise would not save him for long.

A gents toilet. That was what he needed. He walked casually towards the furthest building, realising, too late, that it must be a special high security block since it had a special gate and a ring fence of its own. He consulted his clipboard and veered quickly left into a large office type block. Toilets were usually on ground floors. He was beginning to shake.

He found a toilet on the first floor and slipped inside. He had just slammed the first internal door shut when he heard the main door open and then somebody else come in behind him. He headed for one of the lockable toilets, waiting in steadily rising panic for the man to use the facilities and go.

An arm came past him, pushing the door he was opening shut and the man behind him pressed the cold muzzle of a gun against his ear.

'Well, well, just look at the little Stater I've found,' he said. 'And what would we be expecting to steal here.' He grabbed Jake's arm and twisted it behind him in a vicious armlock. 'Not very clever, are we? We've been reported by three people already.'

They had walked down what seemed like miles of concrete corridors and Jake thought feverishly as to what story he should tell. Should he ask to speak to the Director and tell him everything he knew. That might compromise both his father and mother.

'In here,' said the guard. 'Sit there.' It was a small outer office with Station Manager on the door.

Names were instantly checkable. Feed a false name and an address which didn't fit into the computer and you were blown.

A tall, rangy man stepped out of the office and said, 'Good grief, was that who it was. He's just a kid. Bring him in here.'

Jake was roughly pushed forward and slumped into a seat in front of the desk.

'All right, Johnson, you can go. I'll ring for you when I want you. And now,' he said, swivelling on his chair, 'As for you young man, you'd better tell me your name?'

'Lagon,' he said. 'I come from Mineotts.'

'Lagon,' said the manager. 'That's a kind of odd name, isn't it?'

He called up central register and typed in Lagon and then sat back and watched the names roll past.

'I didn't ask for it,' said Jake surlily.

'Lagon,' he said, 35th block, tenth floor, Mineotts Estate. Lagon Makemba. Unit co-occupant, Ms Leach aged fifty seven.

'She's me aunt. Dad and Mum died and I live with her.'

'Mm.' What are you doing here?

'Hunting rabbits.' Jake grinned. 'Me and the old fox. The old fox got knocked out. Me too a little bit.'

He must have come through at the same time as the fox, the man thought. Still the patrol should have noticed the size of the charge, enough to stun a man. And this was definitely a Security matter. He had better get Head of Security in here. He pressed a switch and asked for Security.

Jake remembered the rabbit. 'I got a rabbit. It's over by the screen.'

'So how did you get to the Station?'

'I walked through some fields and I found a little hut and pinched this coat.'

The man sighed. It looked as though he might have come through the experimental area. The new management were very touchy about that. Even he wasn't allowed in there. The boy would have to see Kurosaka, which was a pity since she was a nasty piece of homework if ever there was one.

The woman who came into the office might have been a head matron of a hospital or perhaps a school teacher by her manner. She was a large woman, of a motherly sort of build with a large bosom and hips, curly brown hair and blue eyes. But the round motherly face was tight with irritation and the blue eyes were cold.

'I think,' she said, 'as Head of Security, that I might have been informed that we had an intruder.'

'He's only just been brought in. His name and particulars check.' The Station Manager seemed to lose interest in the proceedings. 'You can use my office if you like. I have to do the rounds.'

He made good his escape and Jake was left with the woman. She would not be nearly so difficult to fool, he thought. She played the tape of the interview so far and then sat back in the chair.

'Right, Lagon, put on the head set and put your hands on the palm prints on the desk. Then tell me how you got into the Enclave in the first place. ' She handed him the head set from the corner of the table and checked the contacts. 'There have been no breaks in the shield for a week.'

Jake was terrified. The Lie Detection System almost always worked. He would have to tell some truth.

'I was out looking for the black fuel.' He thought of the cavern underground. 'Me aunt gets cold even when it's warm. I make a little fire for her sometimes.' He conjured up mental image of Stick's tower block and desperately tried to remember all he knew of Stater estates.

'You know that's illegal?'

'Yeah,' he said sullenly. 'But we can't afford the proper stuff. There's still one or two pieces down in the old mines under Crater Edge. I got lost down one of the tunnels, then I saw this hole in the roof and I crawled out. I thought I was outside the Enclave at first and then I saw the trees.' Estimating wildly, he made it as far as he could from the real exit. 'I came out right close to here.'

'Mm.'

He couldn't see if the machine had betrayed him, if she believed him or not.

'And now describe what you saw as you came through the Station Area. We know where the fox died.'

It would never do to reveal that he had seen the experimental zone and the dead trees. He thought back desperately trying to remember from his trip through where the plantations were.

'I saw some new little trees,' he said. 'And a little hut.' He concentrated mentally on the hut and smiled proudly. 'Got this coat.'

He was winning he thought. He could see the contemptuous smile. She thought him a fool.

'Lagon, do you know the damage you might have done?' She leaned over and switched the headset off and motioned to him to remove it. 'Those are what we call sterile areas. Those new little trees as you call them have taken years and years of work to produce. They are special trees, not like the ones you see around you.'

He tried looking baffled.

'You know what happens to those who come into an Enclave.'

'Yeah, but it was an accident,' he said eagerly, 'I din't mean to. I got lost.'

'Well, you'll have to show us tomorrow where you came in so that it can be stopped up to prevent any more mistakes, won't you,' she said.

She pressed a buzzer and said to the guard who had caught him, 'Take him to the secure block.'

The guard hesitated 'What about ...er... the other one?'

'Yes, that's true. Damn.' She frowned. 'Use the top secure lab then. It won't be used today because we've got a bunch of ERC students crawling all over the place, laying their grubby little hands on everything. He'll have to see Kurosaka, but I don't suppose she'll be available till late, with this mob arriving at any minute.' She reflected. 'Put him up there, give him something to eat and make quite sure he doesn't get out into the Station again.'

'You were lucky,' the guard said, on their way back down the concrete corridor. 'She usually eats little Staters like you for breakfast.'

Jake thought furiously. The guard, in spite of his manner, seemed quite friendly. He wondered if it would be possible to get him to deliver a message to Stick or Allie in some way. He would ask him later when he brought him the food.

Chapter 14

The ecoscience tutor swore to himself that he would never take this job on again. Never, never never. Not even if it meant a trip to the Enclave. He had had enough.

'Will you stop screaming Kathy, please. It is only a fake spider.' He glared at Snowy. 'And as for you, young man.'

Snowy smiled at him innocently.

Firstly it was the problem of keeping all the little brats together. Not even the little brats, when he thought of it. The upper school students had been even more useless than the lower years. And with the Research Station being so security minded it reflected badly on the ERC if the kids didn't do as they were told. The Director would be upset at any complaints. He could just hear her stuffy old voice. 'I wouldn't have thought it was beyond the limits of even your competence, Finkle, to keep them together in a place like that, especially when you've got dozens of guards at your disposal.'

Ecopro had really done a fabulous job for them, the laboratories especially laid out and working, all good hands on stuff, so that the children could look through the microscopes, drop their sandwiches into the spectroscopic molecular analysis chamber and find out what was in them – the genetically engineered protein rich lettuce had shown the most peculiar spectrum of all, a band of violent reds and yellows, similar, the lab technician had told him to that of earthworms, which Snowy, dreadful child, had thought screamingly funny.. And then the picnic out under the trees.

He was sure that some of these kids had never seen a real tree before. Not close up. The ones in the ERC quad didn't count. Nobody had been close to them for years since they were fenced off behind an electrically charged chain link fence. They were probably artificial anyway although it was terribly difficult to tell these days, fake trees being all the rage. He thought the layer of dust on the upper branches gave them away somewhat.

Their guide was not as nice as Sandy Stewart but undoubtedly knew his job. He still felt a bit upset about that. Poor Stewart had been killed shortly after he had been to the ERC and at one stage there had been a rumour that one of the students had been involved in some way, but he'd heard no more about it recently.

The guide they had been allotted had been more than adequate as a guide. He was actually a benign little man, even though his hair seemed a little darker than the aging face warranted and the children found his sharp zack suit and fob watch rather comical. They had enjoyed walking through the plantations all kitted out in their sterile clothing so that they looked like spacemen, the guide making lots of small jokes and sharing round the bottles of fizz at the picnic with a generous hand.

It was at the picnic really where the trouble had started. Finding out that two of the students were not there, had in fact, somehow, got left behind in one of the labs. It had been really embarrassing having to accompany two large guards back to the lab to locate the missing teenagers. The stupid idiots were still shoving their sandwiches into the spec chamber and calling up the elements on the computer. And had managed to crash the program.

The boy had been quite upset about it. Something lingered at the back of Finkle's mind about the lad. He couldn't remember his name being on the original random selector list. Had he noticed it he would have vetoed his coming. He hadn't been to an ecoscience lecture for ages, he only ever did the required minimum of homework in order to be able to keep his place at the ERC and even then, Finkle suspected, he cheated somehow, although he wasn't sure how. Why he'd wanted to come was beyond him. And then crashing a program.

The Research Unit guide had been quite nice about it. He'd said that they'd only installed the program for the benefit of the ERC group anyway and most of them had already tried it. At least there was little danger of losing the pair of them again since they were both wearing singularly colourful jumpsuit jackets.

Then Kathy had been sick. She'd just finished all her sandwiches and Josta had told her what the lab technician had said about the lettuce.

Then she'd discovered that she'd lost her security tag. They'd all had to search all over for it but it couldn't be found. A really stuffy secretary had made him fill out thousands of forms in order to get her a new one so that she could get out of the gate at the end of the day.

And then everything had gone swimmingly until they were leaving. They had toured the magnetic shield energiser, which was most impressive with tons of intricate pieces of machinery purring in a big hangar with the immense satellite waving at the sky checking the ozone gaps; everybody had been given a piece of genuine wood to take home and umpteen handouts; the guide had taken in good part the reference to dyed hair and then – suddenly – everything had gone wrong again.

For a start there had been the fight at the gate. Over what he had never found out. You would have thought that sixth formers would have known better. Something to do with the handouts. And then the two who had been left behind at the picnic managed to get themselves left behind again. It wasn't as if you could fool the security system here. The gate was on

141

automatic guard. Each person leaving had to feed in a little security tag. The guard at the control on the main exit half a mile away had radioed the bus to tell him that two had apparently not left the building, since his counter showed that 115 had entered but only 113 had left. Josta and Gail had volunteered to go back for them.

And now this. Kathy was quite the most neurotic person he knew. 'Just shut up, Kathy,' he said in exasperation. 'It can't possibly do you any harm. I've told you it's a fake spider.'

'They're here,' said Snowy. 'Look, they're getting on the third bus.'

He peered down the line. He could see the two brightly coloured jackets next to the third bus, as the owners waited to climb on. Gail and Josta must already be aboard. Thank heavens for that then. The guard gave him the go ahead, 115 security tags counted, he apologised again and the buses rolled.

Leaning back in his seat he thought, NEVER again.

Jake, sitting in his eyrie, fell prey to total despair. It was late evening, the ERC buses had left hours ago, and he had no hope left.

From up on the fifth floor lab he had seen the various groups from the ERC walking across and around the central pentagon, recognising Stick almost immediately by his height and angularity, even from up here. Allie was walking next to him, her long blond hair swinging in the breeze, her head bent next to his as they compared notes. They gave no sign of having received his message, they did not look up in the direction of the fifth floor lab, they clearly did not know that he was there.

He had still continued to hope though, desperately, against all logic, until he had seen, in the far distance, just above the top of the security fence the two colourful jackets boarding the buses. The original guard to whom he had spoken and to whom he had confided the message for Allie had not returned so he did not know if he'd even tried to pass it on. He had made it a soppy love note so that the guard would not suspect but Allie would have known. Perhaps the man had just accepted his money and then had screwed the note up and thrown it away once he'd left his prisoner, knowing that a new guard would replace him for the day shift.

Soon, he thought they would find out that he was not Lagon. That Lagon no longer existed. That Lagon was dead. Ms Kurosaka was coming to interview him and she knew who he was.

He was a total failure. He had not helped his father and when they found out who he was it would cause any amount of trouble for his mother. She had told him not to interfere. They had killed Sandy. They had tried to kill him. Whoever 'they' were. The one small smattering of hope he had was that the man in the secure unit at the end was his father, that therefore he was at least not dead.

The door chinked and the man came in who had served him his dinner and left him a thermos. An intelligent, mobile face above a short thickset powerful body surveyed him quizzically. He laid the tray in front of Jake and said cheerfully, 'Ah, I shouldn't worry about it too much. The chances are they'll let you go after a little jaw jaw and a while to reflect on your sins. That's what they usually do with people who manage to get this far.'

He had black vigorous hair springing strongly from his forehead, running along the backs of the muscular hands and arms, and curling over the neck of the white short sleeved tunic from the thick barrel chest. He had a large head for his body, and above the brown eyes, extravagantly curling eyebrows.

'Couldn't you just let me out now,' said Jake hopefully. 'I never did any harm, honest.'

'Nah, can't do that, Lagon. Sorry. More than my job's worth. Anyway you need a special security tag to get out. There was some sort of fuss on the gate today with some kids not leaving when they should have done and so they're tightening up on who's allowed to issue them. And believe me it isn't me.'

Jake's heart sank still further. Even if he managed to escape from this area, then, he had still to get out of the Research Station. He had not thought that getting out might be as difficult as getting in.

'Ms Kurosaka and another chap will be coming up to see you later. If I were you I'd stick to your story and, like I said, they'll probably let you off with a lecture and maybe a fine.'

'Don't you believe me then?' said Jake carefully.

The brown eyes looked at him with friendly intelligence. 'Ah, but I know who kills those rabbits round here, you see, so I'm a bit ahead of the others. And I did hear that Lagon from Mineotts was the young lad who was killed on the train the other day. Of course, you might just be one of the League of the Dead, mightn't you?' He waggled one of the extravagant eyebrows and chuckled.. 'To be honest I don't really care what you're up to. You don't look like a vandal to me, you don't look like a Stater, either, to be honest. And there's quite a few odd things been going on at this place recently.'

'Like what?' said Jake.

'Oh, nothing you could really put your finger on. One or two folk dismissed without real cause, people who'd worked here for years and knew all the ins and outs of the place. All of them Rakia's Folk, though they were dead honest. Been a lot of activity in shipping, this week. I guess it's really since the arrival of the new director that I've begun to worry. I daresay it's because she wants to be the next president of the company so she's being a new broom sweeping clean here.'

Jake decided to test his theory. 'What about the chap they're keeping in the secure block. Surely it's not right to keep people locked up for days.'

'Oh, 'im.' He's not kept locked up. He can get out any time he says the word. He's taking part in an experiment and they need to keep him in a sterile environment. There's a sterile room in the secure block.'

'Have you seen him? Do you know him.'

'No,' the man was clearly unworried. 'I don't know him and only the ones with sterile clearance are allowed on that side. But he can get out all right. He was outside in the courtyard the other day, on the other side of the fence like, but when he saw me he nipped back in right sharpish, even though I was the other side of the shield.'

Jake was in despair. So even if it was his father he wasn't here under any duress.

'Anyway,' said the man shrewdly, 'I shouldn't be telling you anything really. You might be one of those activists going on about experiments and so on.'

He peered out of the window and down into the courtyard.

'It looks as if your interviewers are coming. I'm supposed to be down on C floor. See you tomorrow, or perhaps not as the case may be.' He peered again... 'Best of luck.'

And he was gone.

Jake watched the door nervously. His 'interviewers' were on their way. Did they know about Lagon's death?

He heard the thin whine of the lift in the outer corridor and then someone slipping their security pass into the door. It opened and a tall, white coated man stepped in, saying to his companion:

'Well, well, well, if it isn't little goody two shoes.'

It was Stick and Allie.

Chapter 15

'Quick,' said Allie. 'Put on the white coat.'

'How did you get back in? said Jake stunned, scrabbling with the sleeves of the white tunic. 'I saw you go.'

'Ah well, no, actually,' said Stick, 'You saw Josta and Gail go, wearing our jackets. It was the advantage of the automatic guard. We slipped our security tags in – threw the coats to Josta and Gail through the electric eye and it couldn't tell the difference between them and a human wearing them. Snowy diverted old Finkle's attention while Josta and Gail got to the bus, supposedly with us with them. I don't know how Snowy did it but you could hear the most wonderful screams from inside the building. They climbed aboard wearing our coats, the chap at the main gate checked that 115 security tags had been slotted in and that was that.'

'Except,' said Allie, 'that we were stuck in a perfectly foul gent's loo for hours waiting for everyone to go home.'

'Sussed it out on the way round,' said Stick cheerfully. 'Blocked one of the lavvies, got loads of water all over the floor and stuck an "Out of Order" notice on the door. Worked a treat.'

Stick seemed almost merry. The cold blue eyes crackled.

'And now come on, lad. I've managed to purloin a security tag for you and the sooner we're out of this place the better, before anyone notices.'

'Much he's worried about how soon we're out of here,' said Allie to Jake, 'He's just spent hours on the computer in one of the research offices. I've nearly had heart failure a thousand times tonight.'

'Ah, you were all right,' said Stick. 'It's the little white coats and the computer screen. Nobody ever looks beyond that. Put the light on, do it all in the open and people think you own the place.'

Allie smiled and he realised that their relationship had developed in some way. Stick seemed more relaxed, less angular somehow.

'Well let's get moving,' said Allie desperately.

Jake suddenly stopped. 'I think Harry's being kept here,' he blurted out. 'He's in the sterile area. I think he's hiding out there.'

'Oh shit,' said Stick.

'I must see him,' said Jake. 'People have been killed. I must....' he was sick at heart '... I must find out how much he knows.'

Stick's brow wrinkled. He looked paler and more angular than ever in the harsh lab lighting. 'Internal security is not so bad as the external but you'd need 'sterile clearance' tags and pass numbers, perhaps palm recognition, to get into the secure area. I don't think we can do it, Jake.'

'Too late, anyway,' said Allie, looking down into the courtyard. 'Someone's coming.'

They froze, listening for the whine of the lift.

'It's Kurosaka and the Director,' said Jake, peering out of the window. 'They're coming to interview me. Let's move.'

They raced out into the corridor and into the nearest stairwell.

'Quietly,' hissed Jake. 'This takes you down to Level Four. My guard was supposed to go there, we don't want to bump into him.'

Below them they could hear the series of thumps as the lift doors opened and closed and then the high pitched whine of the ascending lift.

Jake tiptoed to the corner leading to the Level Four landing. He could hear nothing. He hurried past the doorway, conscious only of the noise his feet made clattering in the stairwell, and Stick and Allie followed him, hurtling down the next two flights to Level Two.

Stick stopped and ran across the landing and round the corner to the lifts. Jake and Allie followed.

'It's no use,' said Jake. 'There's no exit from Level Two except this way.' But Stick was pressing the lift switch, tapping his long spatulate fingers nervously against the side of the lift casing, willing the lift down.

'Give me your white coat, Allie. Your shirt is white. Keep going, Jake. Don't wait.'

The lift appeared and the doors opened. It was empty.

Jake was unable to move, standing transfixed at the corner of the landing.

'This should hold them up a smidgeon,' said Stick, pushing the coat in between the lift doors as they closed upon it, and then they were all running again, down to ground level and out into the courtyard. As they came out into the night air they stopped.

'This way for the front gate,' said Stick and then, 'Hell's Teeth.'

There was the sound of a telephone shrilling in one of the distant offices.

'We must split,' said Stick. 'They don't know how many of us are in here. Here's your security tag. Whoever gets out get help.' And then he had melted away into the darkness, heading, as far as Jake could judge, towards a small coppice between the various buildings.

Jake ran too, at first in the opposite direction to the coppice but then realised that he was heading towards the secure unit. He felt completely disorientated. Which way lay the main gate.

He heard Allie beside him saying, 'You head for the main gate. I'll try and lead them away. It's much more important that you get out,' and then she too had left him, her slim graceful shape fading into the starlit distance, vaguely in the direction from which they had come.

He stood for a moment at a loss, chest heaving, heart pounding in his ears, terrified at the silence of the night. And then it was no longer silent as the shattering hammer of the security alarm burst the air and the lights flamed about him.

Without thinking he plunged head first into a small shrubbery beside the path and wriggled through on his stomach as far into its depths as he could, the branches impeding his progress, the small leaves brushing his face and blinding him, unaware of the fact that the spines were tearing his skin and clothes. He had reached a wall and could go no further.

Two sets of feet pounded past, torches flashing in wild arcs as a man and a woman passed him heading for the secure unit.

From his hiding place he could just see the bare strip of land in front of the secure unit, and the two men at the gate, one of them running his hand across the palm print recognition machine and then punching in a code. The gate whined open and they disappeared inside.

They had left the gate open. Without thinking, without planning, Jake thrust himself forward, out of the shrubbery, scrambling to his feet and sprinting across the open piece of ground to the secure unit, sliding through the automatically closing gate and into the shadows of the unit wall.

He stopped there a second, trying to make up his mind whether to go left or right and then had the matter decided for him by the sound of feet crunching across gravel from the right hand end of the building. He ran into a small courtyard which led around to the back, discovering a variety of doors which might have been garages or equipment sheds of some kind.

A guard came round the corner at full tilt and knocked into him, grabbing his arm and saying, 'Sorry. Have you seen them?'

It took him a moment to realise who 'they' were. It was the white coat. He said, almost without thinking, 'Quick, they went that way I think. Towards the main gate. I'll let the manager know,' and sprinted away to the side door to the building.

He ran along the main corridor hearing voices shouting outside, and people running past. The door to a side room was open although the room was in darkness and he slipped inside. It was a sort of common room with a coffee machine and a wall television. Dirty cups lay about on tables and a collection of darts lay beneath a dart board. He went to the far side of the room to the window. He could hear voices outside, a man and a woman immediately below him.

The man's voice was surly. 'I assure you that the man's in his cell and asleep. Or at any rate as much asleep as he is allowed at the moment.'

The woman's voice held the clear ring of authority. 'Just make sure that this place is quite secure. It is imperative that he is not allowed out until his treatment is terminated.' She had trouble with her 'r's'.

'What's all the fuss about then?'

'Oh,' the frustration in the voice came through strongly. 'It seems it's a bunch of kids from the ERC who are here on a dare. They've caught a girl. She swore she was the only one but we guess that there are at least two more in the unit somewhere. Security must have been particularly lax in some areas. One must just hope that they haven't got into the sterile areas and damaged all that work.'

'Well everything here is all right,' said the man. 'He's in no shape to go anywhere, anyway. And it'll soon be time for his next session.'

'He seems to be quite resistant,' said the woman. 'I don't want to have to give him more than twenty units. We don't want him dead.'

The man laughed. 'Oh he'll not die. At least his body won't.

Jake crept out into the corridor and found himself directly opposite the man's office. He was looking in the drawer for keys and security passes when he found the stun gun.

The man was coming through the door and had opened his mouth to yell a warning when Jake shot him in the chest and he slumped to the floor just inside the doorway.

How long did the effects of stun guns last? Twenty minutes. Forty minutes? How many other guards were there? How long did he have?

Jake checked the man quickly, removing his pass card, security exit tag and alarm beeper. There was also a small matchbox sized organiser.

When he was sure that the man was clean he dragged him through into a small spares room at the back of the office, tying his feet and hands to one of the steel shelf uprights, gagging him with his own handkerchief.

Sweating but with cold hands, he returned to the office, shovelling the pass cards into his pocket. Discarding his dirt stained coat and taking a fresh white one from the cupboard he checked the organiser for pass codes. Nothing. They were on a lockup.

Where are you Stick? I need you, he thought feverishly.

Somewhere there must be a list of pass codes.

He called up the main menu on the terminal, checking frantically under first Security, then, Pass Codes, finally finding the list under Buildings, Unit Five. He plugged in the organiser and transferred them, switching off the building's security cameras as far as he could. There would, he knew, be ultimate pass codes which would lock up the most sensitive areas and which could be activated from central control, but these would only be put into action if people realised there was a problem. He set the phone to outgoing calls and rang the talking time service and then left the office, shutting the door and locking it behind him.

The pass card codes were labelled for each area, labs, kitchen, dark room, overnight rooms, even indicating which floors. He ran along the corridors, more and more frantically, opening door after door, expecting to meet another guard at every corner, but there was no one there. He finished, finally, in the basement, having tried everywhere else, at a room labelled Stores. He opened it.

There was a small red light on and someone lying on a pallet bed with a thin quilt over him, a thin emaciated creature who mumbled and turned in his sleep, his sunken cheeks blowing, a thin line of spittle on his chin. As the door swung back the man rolled over and opened grey filmy eyes which looked at Jake without recognition.

'Oh, Harry,' Jake said.

Chapter 16

The man swung his legs over the side of the bed and pushed himself forward to stand shakily on his feet, peering at Jake incredulously.

'Jake?' he said wonderingly, 'Jake?' and then his face crumpled and he put a shaking hand over his eyes. 'Oh God,' he said. 'What are they doing to me now?'

'It's not them, it's me, Jake,' said Jake. 'I've come to get you out.'

But Harry had turned his back on him and was saying loudly, 'Get this thing out of here. I will not cooperate. Get it out.' and then, despairingly, 'What have you done with my son.'

He turned and his eyes were those of the idiot's at Ginny's. 'I know you,' he said, the crazy smile beginning to lift the corners of his mouth. 'You're a figment. You're all figments. But you don't fool me. Headset, no headset. You're all figments. Today I'm not going to play.'

'Harry, Harry, it's me,' he said, 'Jake.'

He put his hand out and touched Harry's arm, only to have him shake it off petulantly.

'Not going to play. Go away.'

It was no good.

'Oh Harry,' he groaned. 'What have they done to you?'

Harry turned and looked at him again, the crazy look fading, to be replaced by the blank wall of incomprehension.

'Jake?' he said waveringly. 'Jake?' And then he slumped down onto the bed and covered his face with his hands and began to sob, huge racking tearing sobs, so that the bed shook. 'Please go away.' he said, 'I've told you I won't say anything. Please go away.'

Jake patted his arm. 'Come on, Harry. We've got to go. Let's get you out of here. Come on, where are your trainers?' He dragged them out from under the bed, saying coaxingly, 'Come on Harry, let's have your foot. There we are. That's on. Now the other.'

He could feel the seconds ticking away in his head like a time bomb. Had fifteen minutes gone by? How often did they check? He pulled Harry to his feet and took his hand. 'Righto, Harry,' he said gently. 'Let's walk.'

He shoved a couple of cushions into the bed and hurled the dirty old blanket over them – perhaps someone would think that Harry was still lying there – and locked the door behind them.

Which was the best way out? He dragged Harry along the corridor behind him trying to get a mental picture of the building, heading for the back exit. They had reached it, he was opening it and pulling Harry through when the alarm sounded again.

Lights blazed all around the building so that it was as bright as daylight outside. He looked at the gate. It was open. Guards must be in the building. The gate would close automatically but if he ran he would get there. But what about Harry?

He put his arm around his shoulder and pulled him to him. He felt light and frail. I'll soon be as tall as Harry, he thought.

'Come on,' he said, 'Just a few steps more.'

Another guard came running through the gate, her stun gun at the ready.

'Oh well, at least we tried,' Jake said.

Harry looked at him and smiled nervously.

'Jake?' he said, 'Is it really you, Jake?'

Jake was still smiling when the stun gun caught him full in the chest and he fell forward into darkness.

* * *

He came to feeling something cool washing his forehead.

'Don't try and move yet,' said Allie.

He struggled and waves of nausea swept over him.

'You've been out about twenty minutes,' she said. 'Just lie still a bit.'

It was pleasant lying in Allie's arms, having his forehead stroked. He no longer wanted to move. He could feel her soft rounded shape against him and closed his eyes for a second. Then full realisation of what had happened came back to him.

He dragged himself up. 'Harry,' he said. 'Harry, is he here?'

Harry was sitting on the edge of the bed settee, rocking back and forth. In the corner was the coffee machine and the table littered with dirty plastic cups. They must be back in the secure block.

'No, please, not again.' Harry was saying, his eyes blank and staring. 'Please, not again. I won't say anything.'

'What's wrong with him?' said Allie.

'I think it's computer wipe,' said Jake sadly. 'They put them into the old fashioned virtual reality headsets for too long. It doesn't have to be anything special, games even, but the flicker on the old sets eventually triggers small fits like epilepsy and in the end, if you do it too often, of course, it scrambles the brain.'

Allie's face was white and appalled.

'It's a form of brainwashing. It looks as if they've been using old footage of me and mum as well to confuse him. I think they'd already done it to a young chap from the Fairfield Estate. In the end they can't distinguish between the real world and what the computer's telling them. They don't know what's real and what's not.'

'Will he get better?'

Jake felt immensely tired. 'I don't know. If we can get him out maybe. The woman said he was very resistant. But I think it will take only a couple more sessions to destroy him completely. It looks like the effects of oxygen withdrawal and people would probably say it was that. He wouldn't be dead, so they haven't technically killed anybody, but he might just as well be.'

'Stick must have got out,' she said, looking at Harry anxiously. 'He'll bring help as soon as he can.' Jake thought to himself that he wished he could be as sure. A smile lifted her face. 'I told you he spent hours with the computer before we found you, didn't I?'

'Did he find anything out?'

'Well we discovered a fair bit before we came. We think we've found out the connection between Runa Seven and pneumycidine...'

'What on earth's pneumycidine?'

'It's that natural ingredient, c1507 something that Harry had marked on the formula for Wheatie Pie. It's somehow connected to cellulose...'

'Cellulose as in fibre?'

'Oh yes,' she smiled, 'I suppose so. I hadn't thought of that. Wheatie Pie, the breakfast Cereal that keeps you on the Move!' She grinned. 'Anyway cellulose comes from trees, as well as certain green stuffs, but if the trees are attacked by a certain fungus – I forget the name – the chemical c1507.4, pneumycidine, is produced. Since Ecopro aren't allowed to use natural pneumycidine they have to make it synthetically which costs the absolute earth. That's why the drug is so expensive.'

Jake thought of all the blackened stumps in the experimental area.

'They've got some dead trees out the back. They must have deliberately infected the trees here as well as in Runa Seven.'

'If you get it from trees it hardly costs anything. You just have to make sure that the infection doesn't spread.'

'Is that what happened in Runa Five and Runa Eight?' He remembered the pencilled five and eight in Harry's notes. 'Almost complete destruction of two Enclaves?'

'It looks like it, doesn't it?'

'How have they managed to get away with it?' said Jake despairingly.

'Stick reckons they must have put back restitution of the ozone by years.'

So the so-called guardians were pillagers. 'Rape and pillage,' Clint had said, 'rape and pillage.'

'We figured that maybe that's what had happened in Runa Seven, that they were destroying the trees and that your Dad discovered it ....'

'.... and took money to hide the fact.' said Jake sadly.

'So why do they need to computer wipe him? ...If he's taken the money.'

'Perhaps he was quite happy not to say anything at first,' Jake was guessing wildly, piecing together the scraps of information which he knew. 'But then the man in Runa Seven died and another ended up with a scrambled brain and Harry guessed that something really nasty was afoot and decided to tell the police, even if it meant he was exposed.'

'That's why he phoned your mother, to get her to check out what really happened in Runa Seven.'

'No wonder she was upset if she thought that Harry was mixed up in murder. Then he must have realised that they were on to him, they'd probably got his phone tapped, and so he sent me the card.....

'....because he knew your Mum would be in Runa Seven and he couldn't send it to her if they were watching her. Anyway,' said Allie sombrely, 'They guessed soon enough you'd got it.'

'I don't know how they can hope to get away with it.'

'In one of the areas we looked at they've got all sorts of crates boxed up, to go out all over the world.'

Jake remembered his guard on the fifth floor. 'There's been a lot of activity in Shipping' he had said.

'I presume they're moving all the evidence.'

'They can't move all the trees,' Allie objected.

'They don't need to. They'll claim it was a natural accident. At the moment it's in a confined area.'

'But there's witnesses.'

He felt cold. They were the witnesses. Were they to be computer wiped also.

She read his thoughts. 'Don't forget, they haven't got all of us. Stick's fetching help. We just have to sit tight until he gets back. I don't see that they can possibly kill all of us. Stick said they wouldn't.'

Jake was beginning to feel slightly uneasy. There was something about the way that Allie talked about Stick, the glow in her eyes, the warmth in her voice.

She couldn't like Stick, could she? So he was clever, and he'd proved to be invaluable in this affair, but he was still a liar, a cheat and a thief, definitely, thought Jake, not to be trusted.

'Stick doesn't know about Harry,' was all he said.

'He won't be long bringing help.'

'We don't even know he's got out. We don't even know that he's on our side.'

'How can you be so stupid?' she flashed. 'Of course he's on our side. He got us in here and he almost got us out. It wasn't his fault that those people arrived too soon.'

'It's not that, Allie.' In the face of her ferocious partisanship he felt that his fears about Stick were difficult to justify. 'It's just that he's not honest, you know. He steals from Sopotos and probably other places as well.'

'Oh,' said Allie furiously, 'It's right what he calls you. Little goody two shoes. And he's risking what little he's got to help you out. Who's going to be the worse off after this little affair if it all goes wrong, do you think? You or him?'

It was unanswerable.

Jake was immature, she thought, brave but stupid. She opened her mouth to say more but the door clicked and slid back and a guard stepped in.

Harry shrank back into the back of the settee. 'No,' he said 'No.'

The guard gestured at Jake with her stun gun. 'Out.'

Jake said rapidly, 'The people who are holding us here are responsible for serious crimes. If anything should happen to us would you please go to the police and report it.'

'Terrorists who try to wreck Enclaves deserve all they get,' said the guard coldly. 'And you'll have the chance to tell the police all about your rights yourself in the morning. Come on. Get a move on. Out!'

'Keep two paces in front of me.' The woman kept the gun trained on him all along the little covered paths and through the creeper clad archways to the control centre. There was no opportunity at all for escape.

He recognised the control area as the building in which the station manager had his office but the man was not in the room to which he was led. There was only Kurosaka, whose eyes widened slightly on seeing him, the large woman who was Head of Security and someone else, leaning negligently against a filing cabinet, inspecting his long tapering fingers. He looked up as Jake was brought in. It was Stick.

'That's him.' The pale blue eyes crackled with the old contempt. 'His name's Jake Delagard. He's Stanford Farnol's son. He knows about the formula but not much else. And he hasn't got it. I've got it. And you've got the card so we're all right, aren't we?'

At first Jake didn't understand and then the full enormity of Stick's words sank in.

'Traitor!'

He was lunging at Stick, hurling himself forward, aiming for the face with its mocking, contemptuous sneer, but was brought down quickly and easily by the guard.

'Careful now, little goody two shoes. We wouldn't want you to get hurt.'

He tried to rise and the guard twisted his arm so that he came to his knees again, wincing from the searing pain in his shoulder.

'And now, I think, if you don't mind.' Stick was levering himself in his uncoordinated, awkward manner away from the filing cabinet, 'I'll take my money and go. Half now, half tomorrow. You'll receive all those little items you were looking for at Mr Farnol's's place from me then.

Kurosaka's voice was a whiplash. 'Get them for us now.'

'Oh tutt tutt. You didn't imagine that you'd obtain those interesting artefacts while I am, if you'll pardon me for saying so, in your unlovely hands. No. Outside. Tomorrow. At a place that I will stipulate. Make sure you have the exact amount. After all, you were paying Mr Farnol a considerable sum to keep this little matter to himself and now that he is unable to involve you I feel that it is only reasonable that you should hand his share on to me. I – er – take up the baton you might say.'

'Scum,' said Jake. 'Filthy scum. Have you seen what they've done to my father.'

Something flashed in Stick's eyes. Could it have been, Jake thought fleetingly, compassion? But Stick was dead to any fellow feeling.

'Of course,' he said smoothly, the pale skin looking even paler in the artificial light, 'Should anything happen to me even remotely resembling what has happened to poor Mr Farnol an explanatory note will go straight to the Ministry of Trade. In fact,' and his next words were a command, 'I'll take the money now and then you'll need to give me access to one of your computers and a phone.'

Kurosaka was frowning, trying to work out how dangerous Stick was.

'And why should I do that?'

'Because my friends, before I even set foot in your pernicious building I left a set of coded instructions designed to send the information straight to the Ministry if I was not back at a certain time. I'll need to disable those instructions from here since the time has run out.' The long bony body straightened and the calm condemning eyes looked straight through Ms Kurosaka. 'I'm sure you'd want that.'

She looked as if she would like to murder him. Picking up an envelope she weighed it carefully in her hand and then handed it over.

'You can use the phone in the next room. Nagasa go with him and make sure he does not leave until someone can accompany him.'

The internal phone tweeted and she flipped the switch angrily.

'I thought I said I was not to be disturbed.'

The anxiety in the voice came out into the room.

'What?' she said. 'Here? At this time of night?'

There were more anxious noises coming from the intercom but Jake, straining, could not make out what was being said. Kurosaka had clearly decided that there was no problem and boredom was setting in.

'Ignore them,' she said crisply. 'They can't get in. It's cold out there. They'll soon go.'

She flipped the switch again and swivelled in her chair to look back at Jake.

'And now, young man, I expect you'd like to talk to your mother.'

Chapter 17

She stood at the end of the room, her hand on a chair back, wearing the suit she had had on when she left the house for Kinshasa. The hologram imager was so clear that he could see the clean cut line of her cheekbones, the determined shape of the chin and then, as she took a step round the chair and forward, the tiny lines around her eyes and her fatigue. She looked past Kurosaka towards him, her eyes widening in shock.

'Jake! What are you doing there?'

He looked at her and tried to say something and found no words.

'Jake is here as our guest,' said Ms Kurosaka smugly. 'Like Mr Farnol. His young friend Allie as well.'

Jake's heart died within him. She would be pressured into doing something illegal because of him. It would destroy her. His mother, he knew, would never be able to live with herself, believing that she had concealed vital evidence, had contributed to the destruction of the Enclaves, had condoned, acquiesced to murder. If he had obeyed her and not tried to contact his father none of this would have happened.

She was still looking totally shocked.

He heard Ms Kurosaka's voice saying, 'Mr Farnol I'm afraid, is in no position to talk just now and I will leave it to you to convince him that he should not attempt to make public his findings with respect to limited substances and Aziproan. Your report goes to the Ministry of Trade Commission on the Enclaves tomorrow. It is vital that any such report be positive on the aspects of Ecopro's activities in Runa Seven. We will be awaiting the publication of the report tomorrow afternoon. In the event of it being favourable we will be happy to restore your family and – ah – friends to you.'

His mother had her hand grenade look.

'Should anything happen to any of my family or friends, Ms Kurosaka, there won't be a Runa anywhere where your bloody company can set up. See if your boss would like that.'

Jake was aware that Stick had returned to the room and was watching the screen with interest. 'Oh, bravo, Ms Delagard, bravo. I do like to see a bit of positive thinking. So refreshing.'

'Shut up, damn you,' said Jake savagely. 'Haven't you done damage enough?'

But Stick was laughing and turning away, exchanging a smirk with the guard next to him who appeared to find him very amusing. 'Time I think I went, don't you, Nagasa. Are you going to show me out?'

Jake swung back to his mother, pulling against the guard's restraining hand. 'Don't change your report, Mum,' he yelled. 'They'll kill us anyway.'

But the hologram was fading, his mother's face losing its clear cut look, her eyes signalling him, for a second, something which he could not catch and then she was gone.

'Take him back to his room,' said Kurosaka curtly. 'Johnson will show Mr Michaelis out.'

Back in the secure block he slumped on the chair next to the table and laid his head on his arms. Nothing mattered any more. He had helped destroy his family.

'What happened?' said Allie. 'Jake, for heaven's sake, what happened?'

'Stick's betrayed us,' he said heavily.

Her voice was high, like a child's. 'What do you mean, "betrayed us"?'

'What I said. He's sold out to the highest bidder.'

She flared at him, 'How can you say such a thing? How can you be such a blind, prejudiced pig. Stick has been trying to help you. How can you be so petty and mean minded as to think that.'

Jake looked at her with dulled eyes. 'He was there. With Kurosaka. He told me. They are paying him for the formula, the photograph, the card – whatever.'

'But you can't be so stupid as to ....' He saw her stop in mid-sentence and then the blood drain from her face.

'Oh, no,' she said. 'I can't believe it. No. He must have been pretending.'

'Can't you see it. He's a liar, a traitor, a thief – he doesn't care about anyone. He was only trying to find out things to sell to them. He's just a small criminal.'

Allie was suddenly furious. 'Oh you're so good, aren't you? You with your protected life style, all your advantages. You've never thought what it might be like to live in downtown Kington without all of that.'

He was desperate. 'How can you be so blind, Allie. How can you possibly justify someone like that?'

'What about your father?' she yelled and then stopped, appalled. 'I'm sorry, Jake, I should never have said that.'

Furious and at the same time frightened, he shouted, 'The problem is you're in love with him.'

Her face changed, became tired, sad. 'And what if I am?' she said.

No, he thought, no, it can't be.

She looked at him, white and strained, the beautiful brown eyes bewildered. 'I think I must have been in love with him all along. I refuse to believe that he is as you say he is.' Then, pain in her face, she said, 'And it wouldn't matter anyway, even if it were true what you say.'

He felt ill. Allie, whom he loved.

Harry suddenly stood up, wavering on his feet. 'Jake, I'm sorry Jake. This is all my fault.'

'No it's not your fault, Harry. It's all right.'

He patted his arm, feeling only the huge tearing hole in his gut and the cold lump in his throat. There was nothing more to say. 'Let's see if this coffee machine works.'

'What's the smell?' said Allie.

He sniffed. It smelled like wood smoke. Outside they could hear running feet, shouting voices, a panicked voice saying, 'The hydrants won't work,' and then smoke seeping under the door and the crackle of flames. They were trapped.

The whole place was a shrieking mass of alarms. Jake went to the door and hammered on it.

'Let us out,' he yelled, 'Let us out!'

Smoke was swirling under the door and they were all backing away coughing when Stick burst into the room. He was bruised and battered, the pale blue eyes blazing in triumph in the white face, the red hair frizzy bright in the light of the flames.

'Come on! Quick! Out!' he said.

Revulsion gripped Jake's heart. Of all people who might let them out it had to be Stick.

'And which cell are you taking us to?' he said grimly.

Stick looked at him amazed. 'We're getting out! Come on!' He looked at Allie and smiled. His face somehow looked quite different. 'Can you manage Harry, Al? I might need Jake to help me with the odd guard.'

'I knew you'd come,' she said.

There was no time for talk, no time for him to say anything, no way to express the confusion and pain raging within him. They were racing to the end of the corridor, the flames leaping behind them.

'This way,' said Stick, 'The side gate the school buses left from.' Allie was behind them with her hand in Harry's, encouraging him on as he shambled beside her.

There was a crackle of noise and he heard close to him Kurosaka's voice, saying, 'What's wrong with the codes?' and another, alarmed, replying, 'I don't know, they're not functioning.'

Stick waved his wrist at him. 'Thought it would be a good idea to know what they're up to so I've set this to the control room frequency.'

They arrived in the central pentangle, frightened and out of breath. The covered archway in front of them was a hoop of flames.

Harry stopped. 'No,' he said.

'Come on,' said Stick in an agony of impatience. 'I've disabled their system and set codes of my own on the gates. They'll never be able to work it out.'

'Don't like this game,' Harry was saying, pulling at Allie's hand, trying to drag her back as two guards came running down the walkway from the other side of the pentagon.

Jake sprinted back and grabbed Harry's arm, hustling him forward. 'It's all right, Harry,' he was saying 'We've just got to get to the other side. If you run through quickly you'll be OK.'

But it was too late. He saw the guards raise their guns and aim and felt something whistle past his ear. These were not stun guns. These were hard guns. He remembered the rabbit's head.

He looked behind and as he did so a portion of the archway collapsed falling, down towards him, burning down the side of his face and right side before hitting the pavement in a whoosh of sparks. It had trapped his foot, entangling his trainer, and as he dragged his foot clear the trainer came off. He could not stop for it.

The falling archway had at least impeded the way of the guards, lost in a swirl of smoke and flame. Stick had Allie by the hand and was running through the burning hoops.

'The main gate,' said Jake thickly, feeling the agonising pain from the side of his face, 'We'll never make it to the side gate.'

They had got to the corner of the central compound and were swerving round, when his forehead was hit by a lump of flying concrete chipped from the wall next to him, hearing only later the crack of the gun. The guards must have sighted him again. He grabbed up a piece of fallen archway, still smouldering, and spurted forward, the main gate in front of him.

He knew that his senses must be quite disoriented because he could hear from the gate voices, singing and chanting. Someone was shouting ,'Save our Trees, Save our Trees.'

He pulled on one of the great doors, and was amazed to find them opening under his touch. He dragged them wide, looking back for Stick and Allie, and saw Stick spinning away, slamming back against the wall and sliding down it. Blood was beginning to pour down the side of his face.

Allie was kneeling beside him, Harry wavering at her side. Jake ran back almost smashing into another guard who had appeared out of the smoke and flames from the gatehouse. He raised the lump of smouldering wood and struck with all his force, and the man staggered and then folded up.

He threw himself on his knees next to Stick.

'Get Allie out, yonk,' whispered Stick, blood streaming over his face, half fainting.

'You take Harry,' Jake said to Allie and with his last remnants of energy he picked Stick up, laid him over his shoulder and staggered towards the gates.

'Shut the gates,' Kurosaka was screaming, 'Shut the gates.'

'They are not responding, said a desperate voice. 'The code has been changed.'

Jake was stumbling through the great doors and then crowds and crowds of people were surging towards him, some singing, some waving banners with Save Our Trees on them, some chanting, 'Ecopro out! Ecopro out!' and then he was surrounded.

He limped on carrying Stick. He could hear the singing but it seemed strange and far away. The burned side of his face did not worry him, nor the lost trainer and the burned and bruised foot. Somebody was waving a banner with a picture of a tree on it, a tall cedar, in front of him.

'Glory be to Rakia for all things green, all fresh and springing.'

The gravel outside the gate was hurting his foot. Someone held his arm.

'He's dying,' he sobbed, 'They shot him. Get a doctor.'

The crowd was pouring through the open gates into the Research Unit, some already shouting for extinguishers and hoses, Stick was groaning and moving and hands were lifting him and taking him gently from Jake. As he looked up he saw that Maggie, Robert, Ginny, were there, reaching out to touch him, Ginny grinning ecstatically, and then Van Rijk was carrying Stick in his strong arms out of the crowd.

A journalist thrust a microphone in front of his face saying, 'Is it true that they're destroying the Enclave?' and Zed pushed the man back, saying, 'For heaven's sake, can you not see the boy's been hurt?'

Jake could see the round faced elder in front of a camera, waving his arms in passion, denouncing the Despoilers of the Earth while Harry stood bewildered in the midst of it all.

Stick was being lifted into a news van and the crew had put their blue light on top to turn it into a makeshift ambulance. Allie was kneeling next to Stick, holding his hand, Maggie climbed in next to them, and then he was watching her go and crying, crying great tearing sobs while Ginny kissed him and hugged him and yelled, 'You did it. You did it.'

They were safe and he had lost everything.

Chapter 18

It was three weeks later. They had just come from a meeting with the Minister and had adjourned afterwards to a small bistro, where Jake's mother was treating everyone to a coffee, even managing to convince Threskay van Rijk to join them.

Harry had said, 'I'll have a stiff gin and tonic, Van, if you don't mind,' and Vanessa had looked at him carefully over the small half glasses that she was wearing to read the reports, and then had smiled and ordered one for him.

Jake was feeling particularly depressed. It was all so unjust. He could not believe it. The Minister had been scrupulously fair but Ecopro had clearly got away with it.

Mr Tianaka, the Chairman and Managing Director, had been at the meeting and so had the Chief Inspector who had dealt with their case but, as the Minister had said, very informally afterwards, she had been on very dicey ground at some points.

It had started promisingly. 'I understand, Mr Tianaka,' the Minister had said, 'that you accept that

Ecoproguardia has been very lax in their security with respect to the Enclave here in Runa Four.'

'This is so.' Tianaka, a smallish grey haired man, dressed impeccably in Runa Three robes, whose power was reflected only in the glint of his glasses and the steely look in the eyes behind them, had looked grave. 'I am informed that the Director had permitted some tree infection for research and then apparently tried to cover it up when things went wrong. However,' – and it was here that Jake had seen the way the wind was blowing – 'I might point out that large parts of the experimental area were completely destroyed by the fire. It is the Company's contention that the amount of infection was exaggerated.'

He had looked at Jake. 'The young man may well have overestimated.'

'It's a pity, Mr Tianaka,' the Minister had said rather sharply, 'that your people cleared the area so thoroughly afterwards. After such a serious accident time should have been allowed for the Ministry's inspectors to investigate the site.'

Tianaka had spread his hands and smiled ruefully. 'With the danger of fire to the rest of the Enclave they felt it was better to clear the area completely. I understand samples of all materials were held for your Inspectors.'

Carefully chosen samples, thought Jake. Tianaka had made much, of course, of the fact that he and Stick and Allie had been in the Enclave illegally and that it was actually Stick who had started the fire.

His mother had demanded angrily if that was an excuse for shooting at children and Tianaka had said stiffly that naturally the guards had fired at people who had set fire to the Research Unit, who might well have been terrorists intent on destroying the Enclave. In fact, he said, they would have done so if the windbreak had not stopped the fire spreading.

He had blamed it all, of course, on Kurosaka and the Research Unit's Director. Both, it turned out, had worked in Runa Seven. 'Ms Kurosaka maintained, that she was being blackmailed,' Tianaka had paused and given a small smile to show that he considered the excuse laughable himself, '- that she was being blackmailed by the League of the Dead.' He added with just the right hint of scepticism, 'We have not been able to verify this, of course.'

Too right, thought Jake in disgust. Typical that they blame it on some non-existent group, some fairy story League, while the real people got away with it.

It was true, Jake thought, that Ms Kurosaka had been charged but Harry's lawyers were not hopeful of getting her convicted. 'Getting these psychiatrists to say that it is or isn't computer wipe is like picking coals from the fire with your fingers,' said one. Tianaka claimed that the head office had been quite unaware of what had been going on and had been delighted when Ms Delagard – a small bow to his mother – had brought the problems relating to limited substances to their notice in her report. They were only too anxious to rectify matters.

'In fact,' he had said blandly, 'it appears that someone from your Ministry was actually conniving with Ms Kurosaka and her team to conceal the damage done to the Enclave in Runa Seven.'

The Minister had smiled happily. She was on much firmer ground here. 'It is true, Mr Tianaka, that our police were informed that Mr Farnol had been involved, that certain payments had been made and sums of money handed over. However, I should tell you that no evidence of any kind was found of misconduct on Mr Farnol's part. No payments to the bank, no extra cash, no overseas bank accounts, nothing. We have been most thorough. Is this correct, Chief Inspector?

The Chief Inspector, a thin greying woman, coughed and agreed. No unaccounted for payments had been made to Mr Farnol's bank account apart from his pay for the past two years. No cash had been found, no overseas bank accounts. The conversations on disk which Ecopro had sent them proved to be totally garbled, computer wipe of some kind.

Tianaka was looking discomfited.

'Where on earth did you transfer the money from Harry's account to?' Jake had asked Stick, recovering in his hospital bed, when he and Allie had been in to see him for the second time.

Stick had grinned wanly. 'Crater Edge Hospital Fund. With that and the money Ecopro gave me they'll soon be able to give people treatment almost as good as they get here.'

Later, Harry had said somewhat uncomfortably, as Stick apologised to him, 'Rubbish, old boy, you saved my bacon. I've never been more thankful to see an empty bank account in my life.'

'In fact,' the Minister had continued, and this was her trump card, 'Mr Farnol informed Ms Delaguard of his suspicions prior to her departure for Kinshasa.'

Vanessa had leaned forward and put a series of documents on the table. She was about to give a skilfully edited version of what had happened but her voice was firm and her manner assured.

'As you know, Minister, the amounts of certain substances imported into this country are strictly controlled. One of these is c1507.4.'

The Minister had frowned. 'c1507.4?'

It's called pneumycidine. As the base of a drug it is a lung purifier. It occurs relatively rarely in natural cellulose, when a tree is infected with a particular fungus. Mr Farnol had discovered pneumycidine in the product Wheatie Pie...'

'As in fibre,' said the Minister.

'As in fibre. Pneumycidine is extremely expensive to produce synthetically so Mr Farnol wondered why it should show up in Wheatie Pie where it had no value. Could it be that it was appearing, so to speak, in the cellulose that they were using for the Wheatie Pie? He therefore checked on the other products which Ecopro manufacture.

'On the night before I left for Kinshasa Mr Farnol phoned me and told me that he thought they were using natural rather than synthetic pneumycidine in Aziproan, that they were deliberately infecting trees to produce c1507.4 since it was cheaper, that they were themselves destroying the trees they were paid to defend. Since he had no proof I wrote a long transcription of his phone call (also considerably edited, she thought, with no mention of poor Harry's terror and his shamed admission of involvement) and left it where it would be collected by my son at the end of the week. Had anything happened to me or, for that matter to Mr Farnol, my son was instructed to pass on to the Ministry Mr Farnol's accusations.'

So that was the important something at the laundry, thought Jake.

'I had our expert check the ingredients of selected batches of Aziproan manufactured in Runa Seven. Some, although by no means all, appear to have been made with natural c1507.4, although it is difficult to tell. I therefore suspected that Ecopro and the Administration of Runa Seven had a mutual interest in the destruction of the Enclave. It was at this point,' Vanessa's eyes hardened, 'that I was told that Mr Farnol, my son and a friend, were being held by Ecopro and that harm would come to them if I reported my findings.'

'Ecoproguardia certainly never would have condoned threats of this nature,' Tianaka had said smoothly, 'We knew nothing about it.'

'How did the company manage to reconcile the tremendous profits they were making from Aziproan if they knew nothing about the use of the trees in Runa Seven,' said Vanessa, rigid with anger. 'And, as it now turns out, in Runas Five and Eight as well. As you know, Minister, my report was on your desk the next day.'

'How did you know to send in the report?' Ginny asked. 'You couldn't have known that Jake and Allie were safe until after it had been sent.'

Vanessa grinned and winked at Stick. 'Stick had phoned me and got me to talk to him on a secure line. He told me that he would somehow manage to let me know if he could get you out. He said if he used a certain word it meant that I should go ahead and send my report.' She looked at Jake and Harry and smiled wanly, 'I've never needed to trust anyone so much. They had both of you.'

'I was almost wrong,' said Stick.

'What was the word?' said Jake.

'Positive,' said Stick 'If I said 'positive' in the next phone call she was to go ahead and send the report. If I'd said 'Negative' she was to pull it and do as they said. Once I'd managed to get my program into their security system to replace all the codes on the gates then I knew we had a good chance of getting out.'

Stick turned to Van Rijk. 'And of course, you turned up at just the right time, sir. I never really thanked you.'

'We have been more than thanked, young friend. I think the Minister intends to allow us to go into the Enclave freely.'

The Minister had, in fact, felt a bit guilty. Looking at the great plain face of the Threskay she was embarrassed that he and his people had been charged with riotous assembly, when in fact several of them had risked their lives helping to put the fire out. It was true the charges against them had been withdrawn but still...

'I think,' she had said gently, 'That you may have saved the lives of these young people. And, perhaps, the Enclave itself.' She had paused. 'We are investigating the possibility that small parts of the Enclave might be opened to the public on selected days for – er – religious assembly and educational recreation and so on.' She had shuffled her papers. These religious fanatics always made her feel a little uncomfortable. 'I hope your church will apply.'

The Threskay had looked at her and smiled and she had been struck by how the sweetness of the smile had transformed the face. And his departing 'Rakia's blessings,' had made her feel quite strange.

'So who got the cash in the pressure cooker,' Harry said gloomily.

'Well I got Robert to fetch it,' said Jake, 'and I left most of it with the Threskay to look after. I took some with me to the Enclave and used it to bribe the guard to take the note to Allie.'

'Ecopro won't want it back, will they?' said Harry. 'I think you'd better keep it then, pastor, for your flock.' He looked embarrassed. 'More greenhouse soil, you know.'

'It must have cost them an absolute fortune all round,' said Allie. 'There's all those payments that they've made to Crater Edge Hospital Fund via your account, Harry, the cash, the boxes of pneumycidine which were destroyed in the fire, all those labs. Then there's the compensation they're going to have to pay. After all, they're settling with both Stick and Harry out of court. Then there's Sandy's mum and Clint and all the people in Runa Seven. They're certainly not going to make much profit this year.'

'Or next,' said Jake's mother, 'Since they won't be able to use natural pneumycidine any more.'

'Jolly good thing too,' said Allie.

Stick had stood up to leave and Allie had risen to go with him. He was watching her affectionately, leaning on the chair back, still a little weak after the operation. His eyes, thought Jake, had lost that cold condemning look. Was that what love did to you?

Allie too was different, not so regal, not quite so sure of herself, blissfully happy.

They left, and shortly thereafter, Harry and van Rijk, leaving Jake and his mother and Ginny.

'What I want to know,' said Jake, looking at Ginny, who was attacking a large ice cream with every evidence of enjoyment, 'Is how you knew that I was in the Research Unit. And how you managed to get all those people there.'

Ginny's eyes laughed at him. 'I followed you. I got into the Station the same way you did, underneath the screen.'

At first Jake didn't understand and then it suddenly came back to him how he had managed to pass the screen. He blushed deeply and his mother looked at him with interest.

'How did you get in?' she said.

'We swam along a little stream,' said Ginny blithely. 'It went underneath the guard screen.'

'Oh, how clever,' said his mother, still failing to see why her son should be brick red.

'I saw the dead trees and thought that they must be killing them deliberately somehow, so I broke off a piece of the wood and took it with me. I hid out in the little hut after you left and then I went down to the central buildings. I'd been into the station once, years ago, with one of the brothers who worked there and so I knew a few places where I wouldn't be likely to be noticed. I saw the guard take you down to the Station Manager and knew I wouldn't be able to get you out if they put you in the secure block.' Ginny's eyes twinkled. 'So I mixed with your school group and stole someone's security tag and got out.

Then I went to the Threskay. I told them about the trees and showed them the bit of wood, and convinced them that Ecopro were killing the Enclave. I told Threskay van Rijk about you and your Dad too and he managed to get the demonstration going. I thought that that would unnerve them. We couldn't be sure, you see, that you were still there or that you were alive even.'

The large dark eyes grew darker and then brightened again. 'And the cameras had just turned up when we saw the fire and then you came out.'

'I think you saved our lives,' said Jake.

Ginny looked extremely pleased. 'Do you think so?'

'I'm sure so,' said Jake's mother. She settled the bill and then turned to her son. 'Look, Jake,' she said, 'why don't you and Ginny go to a show or something, since you're uptown anyway. I've got to finish my final report and then we'll meet up later for a meal. How say you?'

Jake was going to say that he was too tired, too depressed, thinking that he just wanted to go home and nurse his loss, when he saw the expression on Ginny's face, hopeful and excited and a little nervous, the large eyes fixed on him.

'I say it'd be a great idea,' he said.

* * *

If you have enjoyed *The Green Enclave Runa 7* here's the first few pages from the next book in the series:

Changelings – Runa 5

Coming shortly from Parfoys Press

CHANGELINGS

Chapter 1

The body lay some yards beyond her on the atrium floor. Blood pooled and Allie's stomach contracted into a tight knot.

She had still been in the Paseo Nuevo, one of the central walkways of the great Apumanque Mall, when the incident must have started. She had been looking for the Embassy shuttle and wondering if Helena was back already when she heard some sort of scuffle going on in the central atrium.

'I see they're cleansing the area,' a voice had said.

'I hope they give them a good hiding before they chuck them out!' said another.

She couldn't quite see what was happening, the bright sunlight filtering through the great stained-glass roof of the Mall blinding her. People were standing still, swivelling round, looking in the direction of the atrium where all the Ministries were located. She needed to cross it to get to the entranceway and wondered what to do. She wanted to avoid the fight, if it was a fight. The Mall was thronged with shoppers loaded with their purchases from the elegant boutiques and she couldn't see if Helena had drawn up to the entranceway or not. The mass of green vegetation in the central reservation, the giant grasses, the swaying leaves of the great strangler fig, made it difficult to see anything on the other side of the atrium.

Hampered by her own bags, she tried to keep to the edge of the Paseo but a guard, rushing towards the fountain in the middle of the atrium, pushed her towards the centre.

'Someone's stolen something from the Ministry,' a large woman with unnaturally blond hair reported over her shoulder to the man behind her, her voice filled with excitement.

Two more guards rushed past, voices babbled and then a small dark figure clutching a thin brown attaché case was swarming up one of the trees next to the pool. He disappeared into the greenery and another man next to her grunted.

With a shock Allie realised that he was one of the four-eyed and couldn't prevent the horrified start it always gave her to see one. The eye on her side was watching her, but she knew the others were busy gazing at the surrounding world. The man was nervous, skittish, like a frightened horse when its eyes alight on something unknown. The four-eyed had been bred as soldiers before the days of the Species Integrity Protocol, one of her tutors had told her, some manic general imagining that better sight would represent some kind of military advantage.

'Didn't work though,' her tutor had said. 'The psychiatrists say that four eyes provide too much sensory input for the brain and it leads to system overload. The ones who can function at all are usually just silent and,' he sought for the word, 'sullen.'

The four-eyed man jerked his head and Allie saw the movement in the branches above. It must be the climber, only visible now and then as a flash of ragged cloth or a brown outstretched hand.

Each time he disappeared almost immediately into the foliage, just a swaying of the gigantic hibiscus blooms and gourd flowers showing where he had been. The man twitched again.

The child – it could only be a child – was almost at the third level. Without a doubt one of the street urchins, rogues and pickpockets mostly, who managed to get into the Mall. In theory they were barred from entry but some always found a way in, no one ever knew how. More guards were running across the atrium floor.

Allie watched the child coming out of the canopy, scrambling perilously along an extended branch. She was aware of guards crashing into the shrubbery below, shouting and waving their guns. Her eyes went back to the little figure swinging wildly towards the third level railing. If he could get to the railing he would be over and away. A security guard had appeared from the lifts on the third level but he was on the other side of the gallery.

The child was extended to his full length, ignoring the dizzying height, the terrifying drop to the atrium floor. His hand brushed the railing and then fastened tightly on it. He was going to make it. The guard on the far side stopped, realised what was going to happen, and then stretched out his arm.

The four-eyed man made a sound as if in pain, a gun barked once and then the child was plunging down, arms extended, branches whipping under the pressure then springing back as he fell. Perhaps they would break his fall enough, Allie prayed. There was an ugly thud as the body hit the mosaic floor and the man next to her flinched.

'They didn't need to shoot him.'

She was aware that she had spoken aloud but no one was listening to her. The four-eyed man had slipped away into the crowd.

'There were two,' someone said. 'Where's the other one?

* * *

CHANGELINGS Runa 5 to be released in 2017

Pre-order at info@parfoyspress.com

For a limited period Parfoys Press is offering anyone leaving a review of a book by Jaye Sarasin on Amazon a reduction in price on the next book they purchase. Send the review to info@parfoyspress.com